A thousand rounds scythed the air

The heavy-metal barrage shredded the rebels caught in the open. From his vantage point on a hill to the north, Baptiste watched the slaughter.

"They're killing us," he shouted to Bolan, "cutting us to pieces. Your plan has failed!"

"The plan didn't fail," the warrior replied calmly. "Your men panicked and fired before everyone was in position."

Bolan turned slowly to his right, balancing the surface-to-air missile launcher on his shoulder as he tracked the Alouette, fleeing from its strafing run. He fired.

The chopper was in the middle of a climb when the missile plowed into its tail. Sheets of metal blew off the aircraft like paper in an explosive wind.

An Aérospatiale Puma zoomed in from the south.

The Executioner lowered his weapon. "Looks like it's not over yet."

MACK BOLAN®

The Executioner

DON PENDLETON'S®

THE EXECUTIONER®

FEATURING MACK BOLAN®

DEADLY TACTICS

A GOLD EAGLE BOOK FROM

WORLDWIDE®

TORONTO • NEW YORK • LONDON • PARIS
AMSTERDAM • STOCKHOLM • HAMBURG
ATHENS • MILAN • TOKYO • SYDNEY

First edition February 1991

ISBN 0-373-61146-3

Special thanks and acknowledgment to
Rich Rainey for his contribution to this work.

DEADLY TACTICS

Printed in U.S.A.

Now to what higher object, to what greater character, can any mortal aspire than . . . to discountenance the haughty and lawless, to procure redress of wrongs, the advancement of right, to assert and maintain liberty and virtue, to discourage and abolish tyranny and vice?

—John Adams
October 1759

We fight not to enslave, but to set a country free, and to make room upon the earth for honest men to live in.

—Thomas Paine
March 21, 1778

Love for, and pride in one's country will prod ordinary men into performing extraordinary deeds.

—Mack Bolan

PROLOGUE

The dead man moved.

One hand after the other pawed the dirt of the moonlit courtyard as he spent his last few moments on earth trying to evade his captors. But there was nowhere to go. The white-bricked walls of the Ministry of Culture loomed high above him. Had he been able to stand, there still would have been no escape.

His hair had turned white, and his beard was scraggly; his ebony face was marred with bruises.

Leon Drew, the legendary paramilitary officer who'd seen action throughout Africa and Indonesia, currently CIA chief of station in the East African Republic of Tongasa, had been reduced to a skeletal Rip Van Winkle.

But it hadn't been a gentle sleep.

It had been a slumber in hell, his mind overwhelmed by a psychotropic drug known as Acid Bath, which his captors had used to pry loose Company secrets.

Now the sleep was over and he was nine-tenths dead. All that kept him going was the spirit that had seen him cross two continents in service of the CIA's silent wars. It had been a long run marked with secret glory, covert victories known only to the clandestine brotherhood.

The long run had come to an end.

Hallucinations danced in front of him along the white wall. Spectral figures from his past hovered around him. Men he'd helped, men who'd died before him, they were all calling to him, welcoming him.

"Upesi! Tout de suite!"

"En règle! Don't slouch so, Monsieur Spook."

Leon Drew scrambled faster, his mind conditioned by the voices of the Tongasan jailors. Like many of the Tongasans, they spoke a mixture of Swahili, French and English, cursing at him and throwing orders at him in several languages.

The prisoner responded by rote. He moved faster toward the brick wall that marked the boundary of his life.

The two men who herded him to the killing wall wore the uniforms of the First Tongasan Legion. Light khaki shorts, short-sleeved shirts and badges marked them as veterans of a dozen imaginary campaigns.

The taller of the two FTL soldiers wore a *kepi noir,* the dark legionnaire's cap that marked him as an officer. The brim covered his feral eyes but not his moonlit death's-head grin. He was a staff sergeant well-known for the clever games he devised for the prisoners. The staff sergeant was a good sport.

The other man wore a light kepi, just another soldier in the terrorist army.

The staff sergeant slapped the barrel of the FAL 7.62 mm rifle against Drew's shoulder, knocking him to the dirt. He slapped the metal against the man's head, using the rifle as a herd stick to guide him toward the wall.

Though both FTL soldiers carried automatic rifles, they had a more brutal death in mind for the CIA officer—bludgeoning with rifle butts, boots and fists.

The trick was to see how much damage could be inflicted without actually killing the prisoner. Whoever killed him lost the game. The winner inherited the prisoner's private effects—money, watch, photographs. And his spirit.

1

Mack Bolan gritted his teeth when he scaled the outside wall of the Ministry of Culture building, his eyes immediately drawn to the inhuman spectacle on the opposite wall of the courtyard. A current of rage whipped through his body as he saw the ruined man inching forward in crablike motions, his arms and legs dragging along the ground.

But the Executioner tempered his rage.

The black-clad warrior hadn't come this far only to give away his presence now—and to give the FTL another prisoner to play with. One perhaps even more valuable than the CIA chief of station.

While Leon Drew had regional CIA secrets, Bolan had a global memory bank. If Bolan's innermost secrets were uncovered by the Tongasans it could do irreparable damage to the West.

He eased himself atop the wall and surveyed the interior of the ministry courtyard. Bolan recognized the CIA man. The agent's increasingly deteriorating condition had been released to the media in a series of videotapes—each one like a station of the cross on the way to the man's martyrdom.

The world had sat and watched.

Mack Bolan had stood and gone into action.

He could see that the man was as good as dead. He'd seen it before in battle, both covert and declared—men walking around long past their death had come, eternity just a gasp away.

Leon Drew wasn't coming out of this alive. But somehow he kept his body going. It was instinct and nothing more that kept the CIA man moving.

Bolan knew that the COS had nothing left of his mind but an animal's innate sense of danger. The drug treatment had emptied the man's head of CIA secrets, then had emptied his brain of everything else. The damage was irreversible.

Once the drug went to work opening up a mind, it never stopped. Because of its ungodly power, well-trained interrogators were needed to unleash the intelligence before the subject degenerated into a raving idiot and was handed over for execution.

From the intel that Hal Brognola had passed on to Bolan the entire operation had been sophisticated, from the moment of Drew's abduction three blocks from the U.S. embassy in Tongasa and then throughout his interrogation.

The head Fed's Justice operatives had learned that a three-man Western interrogation team had worked on Drew, one of them a CIA turncoat who knew just what to ask for. Whatever the COS knew of East African operations was now in the hands of his Tongasan inquisitors.

Mack Bolan watched the man struggle toward the whitewashed wall. Much of it was stained with blood and bullet holes, the legacy of the Tongasan revolution. Ever since Bernard Wadante, the rebel leader who was now president for life, had purged the country of moderate leaders the Ministry of Culture had begun to collapse.

The once pastoral complex was now the fortress and prison for important political prisoners. And the CIA scarecrow.

Bolan edged along the top of the crumbling wall, noiselessly carrying the black rubber-sheathed grappling hook he'd used earlier to climb up the outside wall. He wrapped himself in the shadows of thick palm tree fronds that swayed gently in the cool East African wind that swept in from Lake Victoria.

Drew was uttering a strange sound, which was almost a growl of rage—rage at what had happened to him. He was aware that there was no coming back from his present state of mind and that he was slated to die alone, abandoned.

Bolan fixed the grappling hook to the outside wall, coiled out some of the black nylon rope, then rappeled noiselessly down the side of the wall, keeping one eye focused on the oval doors in the center of the courtyard in case additional Tongasan soldiers came out of the complex to enjoy the spectacle.

If he had to deal with more troopers, Bolan was equipped with a silenced 9 mm Sola submachine gun, which was slung over his shoulder. Because of its simple and compact design, the Luxembourgian SMG was common throughout Africa. If the weapon was ever left behind in a firefight, it would point to an indigenous attacker rather than an outsider, like Bolan.

When he was ten feet from the ground, Bolan heard more voices coming from inside the ministry building. He waited, expecting to see more soldiers join their fellows. But it didn't happen. High-pitched feminine giggles rose above the heavy baritones of the men of the garrison. The woman was mostly likely an import from one of the bordellos the FTL frequented in town. They'd been bringing the prostitutes on duty with them more often lately.

The warrior dropped to the ground softly and walked swiftly but quietly across the courtyard, stepping behind the Tongasan guardsmen. The CIA man drew nearer to the wall, his shadow marching up the bricks.

"De mal en pis," the staff sergeant said, laughing—from bad to worse. His French was flawless, a remnant of the colonial days when France had exerted its control over the country and wrested it from Britain.

The British had come from the east across Lake Victoria, intent on expanding their lands from Kenya. The French had come west from their holdings on the Atlantic coast, and they'd met halfway in the Tongasan interior. That had been over a hundred years ago, and ever since Tongasa had been a land of strife. Even though it was no longer a colony, it was still at war. With itself.

Mack Bolan didn't care much about the politics of the country. All he cared about was the COS who had been kidnapped, interrogated and displayed to the world on videotape in various stages of ruin.

The Tongasan government blamed it on terrorists who were supposedly moving the captive from site to site, while in reality President Wadante gleefully watched his hired help loot secrets from the intelligence man, filming him with state-of-the-art equipment.

Once the videotaped "confessions" hit the media, the world had given up on Leon Drew. But the Executioner hadn't. They were fighting the same fight, and now Bolan had to walk down the same trail.

Bolan stepped closer to the FTL soldiers, who were closing in on the CIA man like carrion in khaki. A burst from the Sola would take care of the two FTL soldiers, but the Executioner wanted some answers if possible. He wanted to verify the strength of the FTL force that had been left behind in the fortress.

An operative from the French embassy had provided intel on the layout and numbers of the guards, and Bolan had already made a recon himself, but it never hurt to double-check. That was the kind of attitude that had kept him alive so far.

Leon Drew turned when he reached the wall. He could go no farther. He slumped against the crumbling bricks and looked up at his FTL persecutors.

"Now," the sergeant announced, "the American cur will finally die." He lifted his right foot off the ground, the toes pointing down. Then he raised his knee, cocking it for a snap kick to the head of his victim.

The kick never got off. The sergeant fell to the ground, a grappling hook snared around his foot.

Even though he fell facefirst into the dirt, the man scrambled up instantly. Bolan yanked on the cord again. The FTL jailor stretched out on the ground and flopped around like a hooked fish.

The second man spun in surprise, wondering what had gotten into his compatriot. He held the AK-47 in his hands like a club, gripping the barrel. He'd been about to smash Drew in the head with the butt of his rifle. But now he stared at Bolan, readying himself for a swing at the man dressed in black.

"Sorry, pal," the warrior said. "That's the wrong end."

Bolan tugged hard on the grappling line with his right hand, anchoring himself as he launched a flying snap kick that caught the stocky soldier on the underside of the chin.

The contact of leather on skin made a loud clopping sound, like a horse's hoof striking cobblestone. The man's kepi toppled from his head and flipped end over end into the dirt. He went down slowly, but he was out cold, the force of the kick having broken his teeth and jaw.

Before the man hit the dirt, Bolan advanced on the sergeant, who was swearing and lunging at the Executioner, his knife hand gripping a wicked blade. The warrior chopped down with his right hand and swept the knife thrust behind him. At the same time he pivoted and dropped into a half crouch, right hand back, left palm heel striking forward. His cupped palm struck the knife wielder's nose and turned it into a spilled goblet of blood. Like a switch going off, the man's eyes went vacant as pain and shock rendered him unconscious.

The brief struggle had alerted the FTL contingent inside the ministry. They were coming outside, not alarmed, but curious. They thought something interesting was going on in the courtyard.

Like the murder of another prisoner.

Bolan could hear them coming, their footsteps scuffing on the hallway, their mirth-filled voices floating out into the night.

Leon Drew looked up at the black-clad infiltrator. His eyes locked onto Bolan's with a clarity that had been foreign to him for much too long. The fog that had clouded his eyes momentarily lifted. Now, in this brief dying moment, he knew what was going on. Reprieved from madness, knowing that he wasn't alone at his death.

"Where...where am I?"

"You're with a friend, guy," Bolan assured him. "With a friend."

Leon Drew nodded. He reached out to Bolan, his skeletal hand clamping around the Executioner's leg. Then, as if he had finished his mission, the CIA man smiled through cracked lips. "Thanks." Then his lights went out forever, and the COS tumbled forward into the dirt, dead.

Bolan's back was against the wall when the trio of FTL guards spilled into the courtyard. He unslung the Sola submachine gun in one quiet motion, and lifted the silenced barrel toward the boisterous crew of FTL soldiers coming out to enjoy the slaughter. They stopped in midstride when they saw their compatriots on the ground and a black shadow against the wall.

Bolan triggered a burst, and the silenced rounds cored into the first two men, kicking them back onto the steps. The third man unholstered his automatic and fired a shot, but by then Bolan was no longer against the wall. He was rolling to his left as the bullet drilled into the brick. The warrior charged to his feet, swung the barrel to his right and iced the soldier with another burst. Then he headed toward the oval doorway.

Bolan covered the distance to the ministry's oval entrance on the run. He leaped over the three wide concrete steps, coming down softly on the landing and flattening himself against the wall. He pointed the Sola subgun at the wooden portals, but no one came out. Unfortunately for the Tongasans, gunshots in the courtyard of the Ministry of Culture weren't all that unusual these days.

Bolan grasped the cool metal handle of the door on the left. He opened it a crack and slipped inside, the barrel of the submachine gun leading the way. The deserted hallway was lit only by a small glass-caged light on the ceiling. It was a cool, quiet and church-like atmosphere—except for the sounds of a more ancient ceremony that floated down the hallway.

About forty yards to Bolan's right an open door cast a thin slab of light onto the floor. From that room a husky-voiced woman sighed in cadence with a man whose groans were unmistakable. An FTL soldier was reconnoitering the fleshy landscape of a local prosti-tute.

Past the room with the rapture-laden voices was a stairwell leading to the second floor, just as intel had indicated. Bolan kept close to the wall as he approached the room and peered inside. In the far corner of the room was a makeshift cell with iron bars fastened from floor to ceiling with the cell door wide open. Many of the rooms had been converted to such spur-of-the-moment prisons to accommodate the growing ranks of President Wadante's enemies.

A card table covered with cigarettes, coins and empty beer bottles stood in the center of the room. Three chairs were pushed away from it. Immediately behind the card table was a half-opened door to an interior office. Lettering on the frosted glass window indicated that it formerly housed a cultural affairs secretary.

And though the three card players wouldn't be coming back to their game, the man and woman sacked away in the office had no way of knowing that. They were more intent on melting the frosted glass.

Bolan was about to step into the room when he heard a flurry of activity from the second floor. Several men ran down the corridor upstairs, their feet pounding on the polished surface.

"Escape! An escape!" one of them shouted. "We are under attack." Another man cursed in French, while a third was angrily calling for the guards.

Bolan swore softly. Someone had become aware of his presence, possibly by glancing idly out a second-floor window into the courtyard below.

The Executioner ran to the foot of the stairs just as the FTL soldiers thundered down to the landing, their boots pounding on the polished marble. They carried AK-47s with 30-round banana-shaped magazines.

The men came to a crashing halt when they spotted Bolan at the bottom of the stairs. Their gun barrels snapped his way, metal snouts seemingly sensing danger.

But Bolan struck first, triggering a zigzag burst from the Sola subgun. The 9 mm slugs climbed the stairs, then punched through the khaki-clad posse, knocking them off their feet. One of the dying men got off a loud burst of automatic fire, his aim spoiled by his fall. Splinters of stone sprayed Bolan's left leg with a concrete rainstorm.

The loud burst echoed down the corridor and, Bolan thought, probably sounded out into the bar-filled streets of Tongasa, which were packed with off-duty but uniformed FTL troops.

The warrior spun back toward the open room. The overweight Lothario burst from the door in a post-coital fog. Naked from the waist up, clutching unbuttoned pants a year too old for his gut, the Tongasan soldier waved an automatic pistol down the hallway.

Bolan waved back with a silenced burst from the Sola. The 9 mm parabellums ripped the soldier from stomach to sternum and nailed him to the doorjamb long enough to sculpt a blood-drained look of shock on his face. Then he slumped to the floor.

The Executioner caught a flurry of movement from the inside office. He hurtled over the fallen soldier and stiff-armed the office door just as the prostitute swung it shut. The jarring blow shattered the frosted glass window to reveal a copper-skinned woman in a gauzy robe. Her full breasts spilled from the robe's loosely tied sash as she dived for a red phone on her dead lover's desk. The warrior reached the desk first and backhanded the phone out of the way. It jangled onto the floor and skidded across the tiles.

She came at him then, screaming a stream of French, then a torrent of Swahili as she swiped at his face with her long fingernails.

"Quiet!" Bolan commanded.

He caught her painted claws an inch from his face, twisted her wrist and spun her around. She hissed like a wildcat until Bolan silenced her with the Sola subgun, pressing the sound-suppressed barrel against her forehead until she got the message.

He backed her out of the office and led her to the cell. With a gentle push he guided her inside and clanged the door shut behind her. Then he twisted the key in the lock, slid it free and tossed it across the floor.

Now that the woman knew her fate wasn't going to be the same as the FTL soldiers, she looked up at him, curious. She seemed a lot younger now, her heavily made-up face camouflage for the life she was forced into, caught up in a cross fire of poverty and FTL brutality.

"Stay here, stay quiet, and you won't get hurt," Bolan said in French, then went back into the corridor. There *was* one woman in the ministry that he wanted to see, but this frightened lady of the night wasn't her.

The Executioner headed back for the stairs where the slain soldiers were now standing perpetual sentry duty. He fed another magazine into the Sola and climbed up to the second floor.

There was no more resistance. At least not in the open. Intel had told him that with President Wadante and his mercenary cabinet out of the country only a small cadre of FTL men would be guarding the ministry this time of night.

Bolan took a body count. Two dead against the killing wall, three on the steps in the courtyard, one late lover in the office, and three on the staircase. Nine men. He'd been told to expect six.

The intel wasn't far off, but would the woman be here?

Lights glowed from several rooms on the second floor. One of them had been emptied of the guards who'd come running downstairs. That was the room with a good view of the outside courtyard.

Most of the other rooms were deserted and unlocked offices. But halfway down the hall light shone through the frosted glass windows that served as the laboratory for the production of the mind-destroying drug.

The door was locked.

Bolan let loose with a burst that ripped into the side of the doorframe. It was then a simple matter of kicking the metal plate free and stepping into the room.

2

"Who are you?" the woman inside demanded. Even in her laboratory whites she was a stunner. Flame-red hair tumbled to her shoulders in a luxuriant mane. She had full, generous lips, green eyes and a well-developed if somewhat overripe figure.

"Ladies first," Bolan said, emphasizing the request with the barrel of the submachine gun.

And though she was accustomed to guns—she had to be in this place—she backed against her work station as Bolan advanced. Her hands reached behind her and gripped the edge of a long gray table that was covered with flasks, vacuum jars, test tubes, burners, hydrometers, distilling equipment and balance beams.

This was the birthplace of the drug that had burned through Leon Drew's brain like a white-hot corkscrew.

"I said talk," Bolan demanded. "There isn't much time."

"The guards will be here any minute," she said.

"While ghosts can't do much harm," he said, "their replacements could. But by then I'll be gone—and you might be dead."

"What are you talking—"

Bolan cut her short. "It's what you talk about that counts." He raised the barrel and sighted on her forehead, right between her penciled eyebrows.

"I'm just . . . I'm just a chemist," she protested.

"And Himmler was just a clerk. Who are you? Who do you work for? And who's the next target?"

"My name's Stefanie," she said.

"Stefanie Heidegger."

She smiled. It was a grim smile, stalling for time. "It seems that you've heard of me."

Bolan nodded. "Stefanie Heidegger, Dr. Wolf Heidegger's daughter."

"I'm my own person."

"Looks like you're carrying on the family tradition," he said grimly. "Selling out to whoever can pay the freight."

Dr. Heidegger, a Viennese chemist and psychiatrist, had become a U.S. citizen shortly after he began working for the CIA on a behavioral modification program that prepared agents for living under cover inside the Eastern Bloc. Unfortunately Heidegger was also working for the Soviets. Most of his agents were never heard from again.

"My father was innocent. The Americans murdered him—"

"Right," Bolan said. "He just happened to be traveling with a KGB hit team that was killed in a hunting accident."

The case had made international headlines at the time. Three Russian cultural attachés and a prominent psychiatrist were killed in the woods near the Czechoslovakian border in what was termed a freak hunting accident. The papers had hinted that the prominent quartet was killed by another hunting party who had no idea anyone else was in the region.

The act of God had been arranged by the CIA when they learned the KGB hit team was there to spirit Heidegger out of the country.

That had been more than a decade ago. Since then Heidegger's daughter had spent much of her time trying to prove her father's innocence and the CIA's guilt.

And though Wolf Heidegger *had* been working for the Soviets, it was relatively simple for Stefanie's handlers to paint a picture of him as a great man ruined by a gang of CIA mindbenders.

Her handlers were a team of spooks known as the Inquisitors. Stefanie helped them develop the interrogation and behavioral modification drug program that the CIA had outlawed because of its high rate of fatalities among test subjects and the embezzlement of millions of dollars of project funds. Funds now in the hands of the Inquisitors.

Hal Brognola's briefing had given Mack Bolan a good idea of who the players were. Renegades from both the SAS and CIA were said to be involved, but nothing was certain.

"What now?" Stefanie asked.

"Now you tell me everything you know, as fast as you can."

"And if I don't?" She instinctively stepped forward, her hands behind her back, presenting a fetching portrait of a girl in over her head. Bolan saw the warning signs immediately. The woman wasn't averse to using her "charms" to gain her freedom.

Bolan summoned the image of the COS who'd just given up the ghost. Then he reached into a waist-high flap on his lightweight black Cordura combat vest, took out a 30-round stick of 9 mm parabellums and changed the magazine in the Sola subgun. He nosed the barrel toward the red-haired siren. "Then you go down with the rest of them," Bolan said.

"But I didn't hurt anybody...."

"Tell that to Leon Drew." He gripped her arm and ushered her over to the windows, flung open the shutters and pressed her face against the window where she could see the carnage in the courtyard.

The CIA man's body was stretched out like a withered stick of kindling against the wall, flanked by the dead Tongasans.

"You created Acid Bath," Bolan growled. "You helped destroy him. If you want a reprieve from your death sentence, you'd better start talking."

Tremors racked her body as she was confronted by the blood-red portrait of death she'd helped paint in the courtyard, an apprentice to her rogue masters. Her head sagged and then finally she pushed herself away from the window.

Bolan questioned her thoroughly. Sometimes he used his voice to intimidate her, sometimes he waved the Sola submachine gun, convincing her there was a 9 mm cure for her reticence.

With the memory of the corpses spurring her on, Stefanie talked quickly. There was no way she could stand up to Bolan. And though her words were tempered with years of bitterness, the Executioner sensed a certain desire for her to give up the goods. Confession was good for the part of her soul still intact.

She told him about the various antecedents of her chemical concoctions, then with an almost absurd pride handed over a vial of the current strain of Acid Bath used on Drew.

Though she filled in many details of her role in the operation, she held back the names—until Bolan let her know that it wasn't that great a secret. He already suspected most of the names but needed corroborating details from her.

"Who's the Briton?" Bolan demanded.

"What?"

"Your lover. Your controller," Bolan said. "Whatever you call him. What's his name?"

Her face reddened. "Graham Montgomery."

A former SAS colonel who'd trained with the Omani Special Forces and helped them deal with the Dhofari Rebellion and Yemeni raiders, Montgomery had been implicated in extortion and assassination plots after his return to Britain.

"And the CIA traitor?" Bolan pressed. "Who's he?"

Stefanie knifed the air with her hands. "He's not a traitor! He's just . . . *We're* just trying to stop the CIA from committing acts of terrorism."

"Like abducting innocent men, ransacking their minds and leaving them to die at the hands of Tongasan sadists?" Bolan suggested. He waved the machine gun at her. "His name."

"Kyle Vincent."

Bolan nodded. The CIA psywar specialist had left the Agency one step ahead of a covert lynch committee. A KGB defector had identified Vincent as Wolf Heidegger's liaison with the Russians. After Wolf's demise, Vincent had looked for another pot of gold. He'd found it in the daughter, leading her down a starry-eyed path that ended in Tongasa.

Stefanie unraveled many of the threads of the Acid Bath program, and though it was compartmentalized and a lot of it was guesswork, she gave Bolan plenty to work with. In the few minutes the warrior could spare, she poured out the details of Operation Acid Bath in a numbed voice.

Bolan absorbed the information, then steered her toward the communications room adjacent to the lab. When she made a slight pretense of not having the key, the Executioner reminded her of the bargain they'd made. If she wanted to live, she had to give.

She unlocked the metal doors and led him into a state-of-the-art-communications room. It was the studio where Leon Drew's "confessions" were taped.

Thick electrical cords snaked across the floor to tripod-mounted cameras that were focused on a black backdrop. Banks of video decks, tape recorders and monitors occupied long tables on both sides of the cameras.

Behind the backdrop a maze of sectional furniture flanked a glassed-in rack of high-quality weaponry that was obviously reserved for the Inquisitors— Heckler & Koch MP-5s, nightscopes, thermal imagers, sniper rifles, tools of the trade.

After glancing around the entire suite, Bolan concentrated on a wall that was bracketed with floor-to-ceiling shelves of videotapes with handwritten labels. According to Stefanie, they were duplicates. The masters had been taken to another part of the capital for safekeeping.

The labels listed dozens of African, French and British names. Drew was just one of countless victims fatally interviewed by the Inquisitors. All that remained were their names and their wraithlike doppelgängers on the videotape.

Bolan found two dupes bearing the name of Leon Drew. Scrawled labels indicated both edited and raw footage. He slid them into a pocket of his combat vest.

Though he'd come to get Drew out if possible, Bolan was also supposed to find out just how much information Drew had given up so that the CIA could do a damage assessment and roll up the compromised operations.

Not least of all, the American government wanted a sample of Acid Bath. Certain groups were keenly interested in finding out how the drug worked. They had to find out what they were up against.

"You've got what you wanted. Now let me go."

"Not yet," Bolan said. "First I've got to pay my respects." He stood in front of the backdrop and triggered a long, sustained burst. As the warrior turned in a slow arc, the automatic barrage smashed through the monitors, the cameras, tape decks, blinding the soulless eyes that had captured Leon Drew's disintegration.

Stefanie Heidegger stepped back from the sudden blizzard of glass and metal shards, her eyes following the trail of destruction blazed by the Sola. Then they locked onto Bolan.

"One more thing," Bolan told her.

"Say it," she hissed. "Say it and go!"

"Is there an antidote for the drug?"

"No," she said. "Not yet."

"Keep working on it."

"Why?"

"I'll be back for it."

He strode over to the gun rack and removed a Heckler & Koch G-3 SG/1 sniper rifle. It would come in handy for the escape route he'd planned.

On the way out of the trashed studio, Bolan clutched Stefanie's wrist again, practically lifting her off her feet as he led her outside the office and pushed her down the hallway.

"Where are you taking me?" she demanded, her feet clattering down the staircase, nimbly dancing around the slain Tongasans.

"I'm locking you up with someone for a while," Bolan replied.

"Who?"

"Don't worry. You've got a lot in common."

He hustled her down to the office where the Tongasan prostitute was imprisoned. Picking up the key from its berth against the wall where he'd thrown it earlier, he unlocked the cell, pushed Stefanie inside and locked the door behind her.

"Remember," Bolan said to the red-haired chemist. "I'll be back...."

A QUARTET OF TONGASANS ambled toward the front entrance of the Ministry of Culture, past the bright white police jeeps and drab green scout vehicles.

The changing of the guard, Bolan thought, watching from his concealed position on the outdoor walkway of the second floor. The soldiers had come earlier than anticipated. The Tongasan sense of time was flexible. Usually they came in late or not at all.

More soldiers would be coming soon. Bolan looked up the crowded street, which was full of Tongasan soldiers eagerly patrolling the bars and brothels of the capital.

Rattle and drum music and sighing steel guitars streamed out of bat wing saloon doors. In drunken cadence with the music boisterous laughter spilled out into the night, fueled by alcohol, ganja and blood lust.

Through the commotion no one had noticed the battle at the Ministry of Culture.

Yet.

The four guards walked through the entrance. Only seconds remained before they would discover that security had been breached.

Bolan edged over the wall, his black shape now a liability in the moonlight splashing onto the white background. He wedged the grappling hook in place, then clambered down the outside of the wall.

A flurry of yells echoed from inside the ministry. A moment later two soldiers ran back out into the street. A shot rang out, followed by a burst of automatic fire chopping at the moon.

The loud barrage hammered through the drunken music of the night as the Tongasan guards shot wildly to alert their brethren from the bars that all was not well.

Suddenly one of the soldiers spotted Bolan dropping down the outside wall. A stream of bullets scorched the wall just above the warrior's head, showering his fingertips with concrete bits.

The Executioner looked below, pushed himself away from the wall, then jumped for the hood of a white jeep, bracing himself for the impact. His feet thudded onto the hood, caving it in on two sides like deep footprints on white metal snow. He turned once, fired a burst from the Sola to sweep the soldiers back inside the ministry, then jumped to the hood of another vehicle. Using the hoods of several jeeps as stepping-stones, he raced to the long-range reconnaissance vehicle he'd checked out during his earlier probe. Like the jeeps, the Land Rover had keys in the ignition.

Bolan leaped from the last jeep onto the Land Rover, his right foot landing on the sand-colored camouflage roll strapped to the front of the hood—just as a Tongasan FTL refugee from the bars lurched behind the steering wheel, trying to remove the key from the ignition.

Without slowing for a second, Bolan continued stepping forward, his left foot catching the man on the forehead and launching him into the back of the vehicle before he fell onto the ground.

Bolan dropped behind the wheel, switched on the engine and screeched down the street, careering toward a phalanx of FTL soldiers racing in his direction. The waves of khaki parted like the Red Sea as the blunt-nosed vehicle barreled through. Once past the crowd, Bolan swung the wheel hard right, then gunned the Rover down a small side street that led to the forest on the edge of town.

The staccato chatter of machine guns followed his progress, wild volleys of automatic fire that whipped down the street and ripped into the houses of the townspeople.

Without slowing down, Bolan gunned the Rover off the road and crashed into the bush, splintering trees and whiplash branches cutting the air like guillotines, smashing the windshield before being pushed out of the way by the speeding vehicle.

Bolan took the Rover as far as it could go into the bush, then spun the wheel hard left. The vehicle skidded sideways and came to a strangled stop, enmeshed in an impenetrable barrier of trees and clinging vines.

The Executioner clambered out, H&K slung over his shoulder, Sola in his hand, and ran off into the bush, laying down a fake trail toward the east and safety.

The FTL soldiers would close off the borders and be looking for him to skirt Rwanda and Burundi on his way to Lake Victoria, but Bolan planned on doubling back and heading west into the Tongasan interior for the next phase of his mission—a rendezvous with a madman.

3

Morris Shambela crossed Blackfriars Bridge convinced that a ghost waited for him on the other side.

His ghost.

He'd seen it in a dream on his flight to London. In the dream the spirit told him to go back to the jungles of Tongasa, shed his government shackles and live free in the forests once more.

The dream was simple to interpret. He had to change his ways and turn his back on the life he led. But the director of Tongasa's Internal Security Force was a hated man. Regardless of individual guilt or innocence anyone connected to ISF was blamed for the atrocities and the "midnight murders" that had plagued Tongasa ever since Wadante had seized power.

The guerrilla forces would kill Shambela on sight. So would the peasants. And if he returned without answering Wadante's summons, his own ISF agents would hunt him down.

And so, wearing a mask of calm he didn't feel, he continued his journey, changing taxis several times and riding around the center of London at random.

Finally he got out and strolled through the oppressive heat toward his rendezvous in the Temple district. The streets were populated by barristers and bankers, none of them giving him a second glance.

Shambela was cloaked in a well-tailored, subdued pinstriped suit that he had selected in Nairobi before flying out from Jomo Kenyatta International Airport. His clean-shaven, aquiline face gave him the look of a cultured man, a fortunate son like the rest of the Temple traders. Even though he was more comfortable in khakis or police blues, Shambela pretended he was just one more diplomat on the loose with plenty of money in his pockets and nothing but peace in his heart.

LONDON WAS BURNING. Clouds of smog and factory smoke drifted through the capital and billowed above the Thames in a gray haze. The heat wave had struck suddenly, dispelling the usually pleasant weather in London at this time of year. But the cloying heat and smog was of little concern to the group gathered in Montgomery Manor along the Victoria Embankment.

Adorned with turrets, gables and stained glass, the ancient manor was in a neighborhood called the Temple where the medieval order of the Knights Templars once worshipped. In the air-conditioned comfort of a Thameside wing on the third floor sat a six-foot-ten giant who also thought himself deserving of worship—Bernard Wadante, president for life of Tongasa.

And worship he received, from an endless parade of diplomats and trade functionaries at all levels of government. During the daylight hours a stream of diplomats visited Graham Montgomery's palatial manor for informal talks with the Tongasa head of state.

After nightfall their underworld counterparts came to pay *their* respects. Terrorist intermediaries, former intelligence men and unscrupulous traders—all were interested in what Wadante had to offer and were eager to let him know what they were in the market for.

The first leg of the London-Paris-Madrid trek showed all signs of being a success—until news reached them via the Voice of Kenya broadcast that an attempted coup was in progress. Despite the coded long-distance assurances of Morris Shambela that the raid was under control, neighboring African governments echoed VOK announcements that Wadante's control of the government was slipping.

Montgomery had dispatched a team of British and Tongasan Inquisitors back to Africa to take control of the situation, and Shambela had been summoned to London for a full briefing where he could discuss what happened free from electronic eavesdropping.

The director of the ISF arrived on Montgomery's doorstep at three in the afternoon. A butler with a poorly healed bullet track on his right cheek ushered him to a windowless paneled room on the second floor.

The hidden room dated to the seventeenth century when priest catchers were unleashed on England, hunting down Catholic ministers of the Underground

Church. The former priests' refuge made an ideal debriefing room.

Within a half hour of Shambela's arrival, Graham Montgomery, Kyle Vincent and Bernard Wadante gathered in the room for the briefing. Wadante settled his massive bulk into a plushly upholstered chair and, flanked by the maverick British and American intel lords, stared openmouthed as his security chief spoke.

Wadante's mouth seemed to Shambela to be a dark cave of stalagtites and stalagmites. It was a disconcerting sight. Wadante's sharpened teeth had fueled rumors of ritual cannibalism and blood drinking ever since his early days as a Tongasan warlord.

By the time the briefing was finished, Wadante's eyes were burning with rage. "Remain here," the president bellowed, then stood and left the room with Montgomery and Vincent.

Shambela, who had been standing throughout his reports, simply nodded his head.

Once they were outside in the tapestried hallway, Wadante turned to the trim gray-haired man beside him. "You failed me. You said nothing could happen while we were gone." He spoke softly at first, but then his words rolled like a thunderstorm across the room.

"So kill me," Montgomery said offhandedly, his bored voice a clear challenge to the onetime jungle fighter. Though the ex-SAS man looked frail compared to the barrel-chested Tongasan, his slender physique camouflaged a well-drilled killing machine.

Wadante smiled, his anger dispersing just as suddenly as it had come. "One of these days I might try."

"I'd pay well to see that," Vincent said.

"I've heard rumors to that effect," Wadante replied.

Vincent, a two-hundred-pound psychologist and psywar veteran, laughed out loud.

The mercurial Tongasan had a reputation for brutality as well as sentimentality. Neither had much effect on the intelligence men. They looked upon themselves as equals in a scheme, not loyal subjects of a demigod.

The relationship of the three men was based on need and greed, not trust. For that reason none of them pretended to trust the others. As long as the triad had a common purpose, they were indispensable to one another. After they made their fortunes they would go their separate ways.

"Relax, Bernard," Montgomery said. "I'll keep my eye on Kyle."

"Perhaps you should cast an eye back home in Tongasa where my government is under attack."

Montgomery nodded. "It's a minor problem. To offset the Voice of Kenya propaganda my contacts in the media will announce that loyal forces of President Wadante quashed a rebellion, an insurrection led by agents of hostile intelligence services."

"But in the meantime there is a madman loose in the capital," Wadante complained.

"One man or ten," the Briton said. "According to Shambela, up to ten men stormed the ministry building. But our own agents report that witnesses saw only one man. And apparently Shambela's trackers have picked up the trail of someone.''

"I hope it's ten men," Vincent said. "For our sake.''

Wadante looked surprised. "Why is that?''

"Because ten men can be dealt with easily," Vincent replied. "If only one man is involved, that means he's exceptionally trained. A most capable and deadly man.'' The renegade CIA man paused for a moment, then said, "In fact such a man would have to be almost possessed to take such risks.''

"I know of one, perhaps two men who could attempt a hit like that and carry it off," Montgomery told them.

"Oh?" Wadante said. "And who are these exceptional men?''

Like a crack in an ice-covered pond, a lethal smile crossed Montgomery's face. "You're looking at one of them.''

"And the other?''

"He's called the Executioner.''

Wadante's thick eyebrows peaked. "Then perhaps you two should meet and see who's the best.''

"We shall," Montgomery vowed.

"Good. In the meantime, I must inform Shambela that he is being demoted.'' He smiled broadly.

The African head of state turned crisply, strode back into the windowless room and slammed the door behind him.

A bolt slid into place, and then the screaming started.

TONGASA WAS a splinter of land stretching east from Zaire and inching past Burundi and Rwanda toward Lake Victoria, the 155-mile-wide body of water dominated by Uganda, Kenya and Tanzania.

The emerging East African Republic of Tongasa was a country of savannas, rain forests and desert ruled by a succession of Tongasa despots who continued their tribal enmities in the capital city—with warring tribal groups forming political parties. The effect was the same. Whichever party was "elected" via bullets, ballots and terror gangs would then persecute the other parties until the next "election" was held.

The people would suffer. The leaders would grow fat and eventually end up in exile in Europe, where their looted treasuries would help soothe the consciences of their hosts. And all the while a network of guerrillas would take to the forests, build their infrastructure, and then when they were strong enough, attempt to take over the country.

To the more stable East African countries, Tongasa was a burning splinter under their fingernails, razor-sharp and always cutting deeper. The endless civil wars made it impossible for the country ever to get on its feet, and the strife frequently spilled over into neighboring countries.

Even with considerable resources of large cattle herds, rich forests and a promising but embryonic cobalt and diamond mining, the economy never had much of a chance to develop due to the state of perpetual chaos.

After its independence from France, Tongasa's main export was revolution. Tongasa rebels figured prominently in guerrilla activity in the neighboring countries. With enough troubles of their own, the Ugandans and Tanzanians finally put out the fire by recognizing Tongasa's territorial claim on the western shore of Lake Victoria. And though Tongasa's territorial claims extended eastward another thousand miles—this lunacy was ignored.

Recognizing Tongasan claims was a logical step since, legal or not, the Tongasans already fished the waters of Lake Victoria. Tongasan poaching gangs often crossed over into Kenya to prowl through the immense Kenyan state parks. Even with the Kenyan government's policy of shooting poachers on sight, the trade flourished.

There was always money to be made from ivory tusks, or with cheetah and leopard skins. The demand in Europe was always there, and the well-armed poachers were ready to supply them.

This was the bloody terrain of Tongasa, a nation of khaki-clad armies, well-armed poaching gangs and ruthless guerrilla bands.

And, under the blaze of an equatorial sun, this was the terrain Mack Bolan had to cross.

THE TONGASAN SCOUT crouched low and slid his fingers through the blades of tall grass. He turned his hand up to reveal streaks of glistening moisture on his callused palm. Water had seeped from the inside of the blades when man-size boots had plowed an uphill furrow through the grass. It was the first sign that their quarry was still traveling toward the Tongasan hinterlands, an area partially controlled by rebels in the Kesho Dawa Movement.

"Our prey is near," the scout announced, looking up at the Belgian mercenary who traveled with the FTL patrol.

"Too near," the Belgian replied, scanning the bush. "Why does he leave a sign now? The bastard's been damn near invisible for the past ten miles."

The Belgian was a former member of Les Affreux, a group of mercenaries the Africans dubbed "the horrible ones" because of the atrocities that they had committed. The broad-chested merc had followed the scent of war to Tongasa.

He swept the barrel of his 9 mm submachine gun slowly across the terrain, squinting into the sun as he searched the clumps of scrub and thorn. His eyes settled upon a mushroom-shaped thicket, and a second later a hot-metal whisper erupted from the brush. Blood exploded from the cored skull of the Belgian commando as he tumbled to the earth, sliding downhill.

The Tongasan scout instinctively dropped to the ground. A 3-round burst of silenced gunfire followed him, scything through the grass and ripping into his back. The scout rolled over a few times before his outstretched arms brought him to a halt.

Mack Bolan stepped out from the tangle of brush and thorns, clambered downhill, then tugged the bodies behind an outcrop. Once the bodies were out of sight he smoothed over all signs of a struggle.

A few moments later the hillside was quiet. Mack Bolan waited for the rest of the party to arrive. The big man had decided it was time to be found.

THE BINOCULARS SKIMMED over the horizon and brought the patrol into view. Their sand-colored uniforms, high brown boots and floppy bush hats blended in well with the burned savanna grass.

But most of them canceled that advantage by lingering on the edge of the hilltop. Their silhouettes made excellent targets for a marksman, violating one of the primary rules of patrol: don't be seen; assume you are.

Their heavy webbing was laden with excess canteens and enough ammo to hunt down a small army. The soldiers' faces were uniformly tired, angry and sullen. They had been on the march for days now, far removed from the nightlife of the capital, cut off from the watering holes and bar girls who made a Tonga-san soldier's life just bearable.

It showed. They weren't accustomed to being in the field, and when the sergeant signaled them to rest, they dropped to the ground where they'd been standing.

The men were bored, and they were tired of waiting for their long-range scouts to flush the quarry. The sooner the manhunt was over, the sooner they could go back to town.

Their bush hats shielded their faces from the sun as they looked Mack Bolan's way, right at the clump of man-high brush that shielded his position on the opposite hill.

But they hadn't seen him. He was sure of that. His face was streaked with desert-combat cosmetics, mud and sweat from living in the bush these past few days. He was part of the earth, still and silent.

The patrol seemed unconcerned that he might be in the area. As far as they were concerned he was on the run, with the Belgian and Tongasan trackers on his heels. He'd been on the run for days now, and so the FTL expected him to go on running.

But here it stopped. He'd found the right ground to make his stand.

Like the Tongasans, he was tired, but it was a different kind of tired. His muscles were used to it. His body was trained to take the punishment as was his mind.

These troopers were just used to giving punishment, mostly to unarmed villagers in the small townships they leveled with automatic gunfire. In the eyes of the FTL that was what war was all about.

Bolan was ready to give them the real thing.

The warrior put down the binoculars and replaced them with the Zeiss scope on the sniper rifle. He raised the weapon slowly, zeroing in on the troops. Then he moved the cross hairs from one man to the next, rehearsing the way he'd take out the crucial targets in the next few instants, anticipating where the survivors would bolt to when he opened up.

He sought out the radioman who sat beside a trio of rocks, propped up against his backpacked radio, antennae rising skyward. Then Bolan skipped the cross hairs over two men before settling on a white mercenary who was carrying the light machine gun. A bandanna was wrapped around his forehead, the knots in the back sticking out mulishly like a pair of khaki donkey ears.

Finally Bolan swiveled to the sergeant, who was pointing at a map, then gesturing in Bolan's general direction, while his corporal nodded.

These were the key men, Bolan thought. Take them out, one two three, then pick off the leaderless rest.

The Executioner exhaled, his hand gripping the barrel and his finger curling around the trigger, the familiar icy metallic sensation racing through him once again. This was the point of no return. The world was about to end. For some.

He squeezed the trigger. The bullet took the radioman right between the eyes and toppled him back onto the ground, the radio supporting him like a turtle shell. One of the Tongasans looked up, frowning, at the zipping sound he'd just heard.

Bolan's second shot hit the merc with the LMG in the chest. The gunner had sensed something and was already lifting his weapon. But he froze for a moment while he searched for the enemy and was taken out of the play. The LMG dropped from his hands, and he tumbled into the grass.

Another man dived for the LMG, seeing it as his ticket for salvation. While he was in midair another bullet sliced through the air, then through him. He came down dead, his face thumping into the grass, the LMG tumbling downhill like a cursed metallic talisman.

The sergeant stood, shouting, ready to direct his men, but Bolan sat him down with a well-aimed shot, having tracked the man's rising form until the cross hairs bore down on his heart.

When the sergeant fell, the others quickly sprang to their feet. Though they had Bolan outnumbered and outgunned, they panicked. The quarry had turned on them. This was no longer a safari; it was a war.

Bolan slung the H&K and swept the Sola subgun in a lethal figure eight, taking out four men as they began their retreat. Two others dropped, wounded, instinctively aiming their gunfire at his position. The angle of fire was fairly obvious. It had to be coming from the opposite hillside.

The Executioner studded the grassy ridge on full-auto, silencing the wounded gunners. The remainder of the patrol regrouped, backed up toward the hilltop and took aim at the hillside where it knew its enemy lay hidden.

For a moment the ground around Bolan was alive with small eruptions of soil as a steady stream of lead poured into the brush where he had first opened fire. Branches snapped off the bushes and foliage and bark fell to the ground, but Bolan remained uninjured.

The blood was pumping through Bolan's veins as he zigzagged downhill through the scrub brush. When he came to the gully at the bottom of the hill, he rammed another magazine into the subgun.

He emerged from cover just as the last stragglers of the patrol reached the top of the hill. A quick burst of 9 mm slugs eliminated the final threat.

Silence shrouded the killing ground once again.

Bolan paused to reload the H&K, then reslung it over his shoulder, while he carried the Sola subgun at his side. He skirted the hill, then stepped into a low forest of acacia and thorn trees he'd reconned earlier.

The trees suddenly sprang to life as a group of guerrillas moved out from cover and stood staring at the Executioner. One of the guerrillas stepped forward. He was a massive man with huge biceps straining at the short sleeves of his camou shirt. He had the coloring and regal bearing of an ancient Turkana king.

And the American was in his kingdom.

The guerrilla leader advanced within three feet of Bolan, apparently oblivious to the submachine gun pointed his way.

"Jean-Claude Baptiste?" Bolan asked unnecessarily. It could be no one else. The man with whom Bolan was supposed to rendezvous had a river of scar tissue encircling his neck, a souvenir left by an FTL machete that had slashed at his head during a jungle skirmish. Baptiste had survived miraculously, despite the torrents of blood that had gushed from the gaping wound.

The huge man raised his eyebrows. "I'm Baptiste. And you are the man called Blanski?"

Bolan nodded.

Baptiste smiled, the tension lessened somewhat, but the grim-faced guerrillas who surrounded Bolan didn't share their leader's enthusiasm. The Executioner scanned the faces, looking each man in the eye— measuring and mirroring the strength he saw glinting in their gazes. They were hardened soldiers of Baptiste's Kesho Dawa Movement. Loosely translated, the words meant "tomorrow's medicine" or "tomorrow's cure." Baptiste's vision of Tongasa was a tolerant mixture of Christian-tinted animism, a vision that would promote healing in all of the factions in Tongasa.

"How long have you been here?" Bolan asked.

The guerrilla leader shrugged. "We've been watching you throughout your battle with the FTL jackals."

"You could have lent a hand," Bolan said dryly.

"Oh, but we did," Baptiste replied.

"How's that?" Bolan said.

"We didn't kill you."

"I appreciate that." Bolan nodded at the 9 mm Sola in his hand. "Tell your men to lower their weapons and I might return the favor."

4

The Alouette III scout helicopter dropped from the sky like an eagle that had caught sight of its prey. It hovered just above the tree line, the downwash from the rotors whipping through the dense forest. A gray-helmeted spotter in the open cabin door tracked a 7.62 mm minigun from left to right, searching for the enemy. The copilot sat next to him, sweeping the ground with his binoculars and directing the pilot.

Masking itself in the clearings and then popping up over the treetops, the Alouette conducted a methodical search of the sector of forest bisected by a wide, muddy stream. But the watchers in the aircraft saw nothing. After scanning the forest for what seemed to be an eternity, they moved south.

As the sound of the rotors faded away, Mack Bolan moved again. He lowered his Heckler & Koch sniper rifle, which had been tracking the Alouette, and exhaled deeply, echoing the breaths of the Kesho Dawa guerrillas around him who suddenly came back to life and emerged from cover. They'd frozen where they stood, half expecting to be cut down by gunfire from above.

Baptiste lowered his carbine and slung it around his shoulder as he approached Bolan. "Looks like you've pissed off His Excellency but good," he said, his stonelike Buddha face splitting into a wide grin. "That was the fourth copter today that came within chopping distance."

"I noticed," the warrior replied, "and I don't like it any more than you."

Like the others, he'd been tempted to shoot at the aircraft. It could have been a clean kill. All of their firepower could have picked off the crew and probably brought it down. But the instinct for survival kept them from pulling the triggers.

The Alouettes weren't alone in their search for Bolan and the guerrillas. They were spotters for the troop-carrying Aérospatiale Pumas that had often been sighted in the distance.

The Pumas were conducting eagle patrols, landing in clearings to drop troops off, then picking them up at another rendezvous point. And all the while the Alouettes were sweeping the sea of green, ready to home in on the rebels.

The Tongasan government was taking Bolan a lot more seriously now, sending out the heavy guns to run him down. Almost all their mobile strike force was in the field.

One chopper they might have been able to take care of. But if even one was knocked from the sky the rest of the strike force would come in and do a recon by gunfire. With thousands of rounds in the choppers at their disposal, they just might find something.

Baptiste's group was traveling light. The Stingers, SA-7s and Grails that could knock out the helicopters were kept at one of their main caches, a cache Bolan thought would reflect the evolution of all the surface-to-air-missiles provided by an international who's who of suppliers to successions of Tongasan governments.

Even traveling light, the guerrillas were making less time than they had hoped. Baptiste's scouts moved ahead of the guerrilla band, looking for the eagle patrols. At the same time the rest of the guerrillas had to scan the skyline for signs of the Alouettes before they risked crossing some of the clearings.

It was a long and slow process. Stop and go. Seek cover when the copters drifted nearby. Take aim...and then start all over again. The afternoon heat added to the struggle, bathing the men in a steady stream of sweat.

Once they were on the move again, Bolan paced himself with Baptiste, who had obviously grown used to moving through the shadows.

As they approached the stream the choppers had been using as a landmark during their search, Bolan noticed how easily Baptiste moved his powerful bulk through the clinging underbrush. He moved with a surprising grace and speed. That, combined with the mind of a scholar, made him a potent foe of Wadante's regime.

Before the civil war Jean-Claude Baptiste had been one of the most prominent lecturers in the Tongasan university system. Once the trouble started and Wadante purged the country of all those he considered threats, Baptiste could easily have left the country and found profitable work in exile. But he chose to stay and fight and, unless the right kind of help came, probably die.

Baptiste signaled his men to stop when they reached the edge of the forest. Then, in ones and twos, the Kesho Dawa team spread out, searching the opposing bank before they crossed the waist-high stream.

"Must be a hell of a price on your head by now," Baptiste said as he and Bolan waited at the tree line. "If a man wants to find some treasure, he only has to look neck-deep." The Tongasan leader made a chopping motion with his hand, mimicking the kind of machete blow that had left its scar tattooed around his neck.

"Most treasures come with a curse," Bolan replied. "It's usually fatal to the one who goes looking for it."

Baptiste laughed. "Your head rests easily while you are with me, Monsieur Blanski," he said. "I trust every one of these men with me. Otherwise I'd kill them myself. But it's my people in the cities we must be concerned about. Most of them are loyal, but if one of them sees a way of making money and getting out of the country at the same time, who can say what might happen?"

"You're telling me not to trust any of your contacts once we get to the rendezvous?"

Baptiste nodded. Then he looked at the other side of the stream. Most of his people had already crossed.

"Let's move. In less than one week you can go fishing on Lake Victoria."

"You make it sound like a cakewalk."

"It is," Baptiste replied. "Compared to some other walks I've gone on. And judging from the looks of things, some of the trails you've gone down."

"Yeah," Bolan said. "You've got that right."

"Seen one jungle, you've seen them all?"

"In some ways," Bolan agreed. "They're all beautiful in the beginning, but you're always glad to leave them behind."

"We've been thinking that way for a year now," he said.

"Then it'll look mighty nice when we get you out."

Baptiste nodded. The leader of the guerrillas had been offered help before, and he'd been left behind before. The American embassy had been closed down—shortly after they promised to help—and Leon Drew, the one man Baptiste trusted beyond doubt, was dead.

Now he had to transfer the trust to the man he knew as Striker. Bolan knew that even though the two of them got on well enough so far, Baptiste wasn't about to put his faith in a covert Santa Claus until he saw the supply sled streaming across the sky.

Still, Bolan was the only game in town. If help came, it would probably come from the Americans. The French embassy was a chimera. Sometimes a lion sometimes a lamb, no one knew what to expect from the French. Although logically they would be on Baptiste's side, logic had little weight in Tongasa.

Bolan and Baptiste crossed the muddy water at the narrowest point, then caught up with the rest of the band. Then, always looking ahead and behind them, the Kesho Dawa troops moved like an underground stream of khaki beneath the jungle boughs above.

Though they were a strange mixture of farmers, laborers, technicians, ex-FTL soldiers and soldier scholars like Baptiste, the guerrillas had forged themselves into a strong alliance that submerged their differences for the cause.

Whenever the guerrillas stopped, Bolan listened to them talk among themselves, trying to learn as much about them as he could. Many had animist beliefs and saw the animals of the jungle as their totems, mimicking in their movements the spirits they believed were traveling with them.

It was as viable a religion as any, Bolan thought. Nature gods were all around. If they had to pray to something, they might as well see it in something close.

Bolan kept up with them easily, and for that he won their respect. He wasn't a tourist. He was real, like them, flesh and blood. And like them, he was a target of the FTL.

Ever since the FTL patrol had been taken out, the Tongasan wilds were crawling with airborne eagle patrols. Chances were that before too long the guerrillas would find the talons closing in on them.

But not today, Bolan thought as dusk faded away and darkness swallowed most of the forest. They made camp by a deep gully that followed a grassy rift through the high trees in a natural trench formation.

They scooped out pockets in the sides of the trench, sheathing them with long grass, and then settled in for the night while a quartet of guards drifted quietly on the perimeter.

Bolan took out several lightweight LRRP rations from the flaps of his combat vest and distributed them to the men. Once the pouches were mixed with water from their canteens, the lurp feast brought a chorus of approval from Baptiste's soldiers. In turn they passed some strips of dried beef his way, along with the mangoes, papayas and bananas they'd gathered from the forest during their patrol.

From his left Bolan saw the guerrilla chieftain open up a small metal flask of brandy. "Welcome to the Tongasa Hilton," Baptiste said, passing the alcoholic beverage to Bolan. The Executioner took a small sip of the brandy, savoring the kick of warmth, then passed the flask on to the next man. Each guerrilla in turn took a small sip, then passed it on. The brandy wasn't enough to get anyone drunk, or even do more than warm their throat for a moment. But it was like a communion just the same, each man savoring the small taste of civilization.

Baptiste and Bolan talked in hushed tones throughout the night, mentally covering the ground the guerrillas would soon have to travel. The guerrilla leader covered the strengths of his people, their weaknesses, their dreams. In turn, Bolan made an assessment of their abilities, judging as best he could how well they'd handle any weapons he might be able to supply.

As he talked, the warrior noticed a trio of men sitting across from them on the other side of the gully. Their positions hadn't been accidental. The man in the middle had been near Bolan most of the day.

He was a tall man, not heavy or broad-shouldered, but powerful just the same. Because of his finely muscled long legs and arms, he was almost always in striking distance. He was called Ico—whether that was derived from Icon because of his statuelike countenance and his habitual silence, Bolan wasn't sure. But he did know one thing: he was being cased. Ico's eyes glared as they bore down on the Executioner, practically measuring him for a coffin.

While Baptiste was explaining the limits and capacities of his people, Bolan tapped the man's wrist and glanced sidelong at Ico. "Am I going to have to take him on before this march is over?"

Baptiste's eyes hardened. "What makes you say that?"

Bolan shrugged. "He looks like he's itching to move on me. If he decides to scratch that itch, I'll take him down. I don't play games."

"Ico's a good man."

"So what's his problem?"

"Guess I'll have to find out." Baptiste pushed himself off the cleft in the ravine and waded through the thick grass to the other side of the gully.

He spoke softly to Ico, who uttered some sharp words just out of Bolan's hearing. He would have continued protesting, but Baptiste knifed the air with his hand. His index and forefinger curled into a claw that was half blessing, half strike. Priest or punisher, the choice was Ico's.

The tall, lanky guerrilla suddenly stopped talking. He nodded, then listened to Baptiste.

When the chieftain rejoined Bolan, there was no trace of anger in his eyes. The threat of violence had gone just as quickly as it had arisen.

Bolan arched his eyebrows. "What did he say?"

"He understands now," Baptiste said. "He said from now on he will protect me as well as you with equal intensity."

The warrior smiled. "So he'll still keep an eye on me, but now it'll be a benevolent one."

"Exactly. Now let's get back to business."

The business was Baptiste's support network in the capital city of Tongasa as well as several small villages throughout the country. Without help from the outside, the Kesho Dawa Movement had enough manpower and arms caches to launch only a few limited strikes against Wadante's regime.

Baptiste had established several different cells. Many of them worked independently of one another, recruiting villagers and disgruntled soldiers from the Tongasan army, but it was a slow and deadly process. The FTL troops were always trying to infiltrate the movement. Each deserter went through a lengthy vetting process.

Then there were the core groups like the one traveling with Baptiste, men he could trust implicitly. Those units were few, but by operating across the country they made their numbers seem more wide-spread.

As Bolan digested the information that Baptiste was willing to share, even with the chieftain's necessary optimism, he realized the Kesho Dawa Movement was walking the razor's edge. And with all of the funds and troops at his hand, President Wadante was holding the razor.

Baptiste needed Bolan to even the odds. But first the Executioner needed Baptiste to help him exfiltrate the country, link up with Brognola and try to abort the Acid Bath teams in Europe. Then he and the big Fed could coordinate their assistance to the Kesho Dawa troops.

During a lull in their talks, Bolan looked up through the treetops at the sky, which was studded with stars. With the hissing and scrambling nocturnal breath of the forest around him, it felt as beautiful and primitive as it must have thousands of years ago. He knew the folklore of the region and the lore of the scientists. At least in this area they agreed. Many of them considered the fertile region of Kenya, Tongasa and Uganda as the probable cradle of mankind.

Did primitive man lie here one day? he wondered. And was there war then?

The answer was the same. Yeah, there was always war. And there was always a need for a man like the Executioner.

He watched the skies some more, almost hypnotized by the sight—until one of the stars moved. A light was moving in the distance, and it was joined by another light off to the right.

Another helicopter patrol was looking for them. It was more of a psychological operation than anything else. The choppers didn't have much chance of finding them in the dark. But it was designed to get on their nerves. It was a message that from now on the FTL was searching for them night and day.

Baptiste spotted the chopper at about the same time. "They're trying to spoil your fishing trip," he said. "If they keep this up, it'll be a long time before we get you out of here."

Bolan nodded. "They'll limit our movements with the choppers, increase the patrols and most likely send in a large strike force. Unless we do something about it soon, they'll kill everything that moves in the forest."

"What can we do about it, Blanski?" Baptiste asked. "What do you suggest?"

"This cache of yours," Bolan said. "How far is it from here?"

"It can be reached by noon tomorrow," Baptiste said. "If we have to."

"We have to. You've got SAMs there?"

"Yes."

"And men who know how to use them?"

"Some," Baptiste replied.

"Good. Then we'll reach it by tomorrow."

"But even so," Baptiste protested, "I don't see how that gets you out of here."

Bolan looked at the bright lights of the choppers moving in the distance. "We'll hitch a ride."

Baptiste laughed. "And if the FTL doesn't go along with your suggestion?"

"We'll deal with that if and when we have to. Tell me about the terrain where the cache is. Do you know the area well?"

"Too well. In fact, I spent many years there. Some people say wasted. It's a place that harbors many memories."

"What is it?"

"Before the FTL struck, it used to be a university where I taught my people. Then it became a graveyard. Now it's reclaimed by the forest and haunted by the people who listened to me tell them they would be safe there."

"But you still go there?"

"Their voices are still calling me," Baptiste replied.

"They're still calling *us*."

5

Ancient Tongasan ruins crept out of the forest, the towers and walkways overrun by vines and weeds. Entire sections of wall had tumbled to the ground. In the center of the ruins sat two larger buildings, their shells more or less intact.

Despite the look of antiquity etched upon the ruins, they were actually quite recent. Not too far in the past the University of Tongasa had been located here. Back then it had been a self-sustaining complex with several agricultural projects that employed local labor and taught them skills to bring this part of the country into the twentieth century. But now the farms were overgrown with forest, the croplands had vanished and the country had been propelled back into the Dark Ages.

Roads that once connected the university to the outside world were just crater-pocked trails that led to nowhere. During Wadante's purge of intellectuals, politicians, soldiers and workers, the FTL had leveled all of the villages in the area, killing the locals where they stood or dragging them away to the capital for interrogation, torture and death.

No one ever came back from those interrogations.

Bleached skulls watched eyelessly as the sweat-soaked guerrillas emerged from the thick forests. Remnants of the souls left behind during the first FTL purges, the skulls and skeletons had become part of the forest, like piles of stones and trunk roots. The guerrillas were used to the sight. To Bolan they were a sharp reminder of the future that awaited the rest of Tongasa unless Baptiste's forces overthrew the current regime.

After scanning the area with his Sola submachine in hand, Bolan stopped near a pile of skulls mounted symmetrically on top of one another. They reminded him of cannonball stacks on old Civil War battlefields. Hundreds of other bones were scattered around in random piles, their thin skeletal arms and legs sprinkled through the brush like kindling.

"Looks like you've met my students." Baptiste had drawn up behind the warrior.

"Looks like school's out forever," Bolan replied. Though the forest had crept up on the abandoned site, it wasn't quite as dense here and the lush canopy didn't completely block out the sky. Sunlight streaked through the gaps in the treetops to shine brightly on the skulls. "Why haven't they been buried?"

Baptiste shrugged. "Perhaps there was no time. Perhaps it would have given away our presence to the FTL. Their patrols check the area frequently."

The Executioner nodded, but he wasn't convinced. There had to be another reason why the skulls were spread about. As he watched the Kesho Dawa guerrillas fan out over the complex that served as one of their largest arms caches, he noticed a faraway look in Baptiste's eyes. "Perhaps there's another reason," Bolan suggested.

Baptiste nodded.

"Perhaps it's a reminder of what happened here," Bolan said. "So your people won't let it happen again. And perhaps it's a reminder of what you think of as your personal guilt."

Baptiste looked down at the assembly of skulls, his deep voice growing solemn, as if they could still hear. "I told them not to worry, that a madman like Wadante couldn't possibly gain support. I told them that while I was in the capital, I would use my contacts to put Wadante away for good. And now I must tell them once more that their spirits will be free when Wadante falls."

Ico moved from the bush behind them. For a change the tall bodyguard's eyes weren't on Bolan or Baptiste, but on the pile of skulls. He nodded at the bones, almost in greeting.

Bolan moved on, feeling like an eavesdropper. He didn't disagree with their position. He just thought the less contact with the dead the better. It could be contagious in a region like this.

A few minutes later Baptiste and Ico caught up with him and they joined the rest of the guerrillas filtering out of the forest in ones and twos and moving onto the concourse. Craters were punched out of the walkways, forming a maze of jagged pits.

There was still some glass remaining in the upper windows, shards that reflected the sunlight, but most of them had been shot out from the assaults on the campus.

They headed toward a former lecture hall that had been reduced to heaps of rubble. Beneath the hall were a network of tunnels that served as caches for Kesho Dawa arms and equipment. As well as automatic weapons and canisters of ammo, a variety of SAMs were stacked against one of the cavern walls like a picket fence—Grails, Stingers, Dragons, the works. Bolan reached down and examined one of the Stingers.

"Who knows how to work one of these?" he asked.

Ico, who had quietly fallen in behind him, muttered under his breath about it being a matter of just pulling the trigger. A few of the other men were obviously more familiar with the surface-to-air missiles.

With a nod from Baptiste, Bolan called the men together to plan their defense of the complex. "All right," he announced. "School's in session."

THE ALLOUETTES CAME in fast and low, streaking straight for the Kesho Dawa fortress. On their previous run they'd drawn fire, a few wild bursts that gave away the presence of the guerrillas on the campus. If not for the gunfire, the choppers might have continued on their way.

They'd passed over the jungle-shrouded college several times without incident—until the ineffectual rounds came their way from some guerrillas who couldn't help triggering bursts. After radioing their position to the Puma troop transport helicopters, the Alouette pilots turned back to pin down the rebels until the FTL air mobile force came in.

After a dead-on approach to the shattered remains of the university complex, the tail chopper dropped out of sight and the lead veered to the right, heading for the tallest structure, a multistoried science building.

Automatic gunfire ripped from the crumbling rooftop as the chopper drew near, and streams of lead flew up from the ground cover where another group of rebels waited. The barrage smacked into the armored sides of the helicopter like hard metal rain, but then buzzed harmlessly past as the aircraft completed its turn and circled away from the structure.

Then the Alouette bore down for its softening-up run, launching two rockets at the top of the tower. Gray plumes etched across the bright afternoon sky, marking the path of the twin wire-guided missiles. They struck almost simultaneously, punching through the granite-and-concrete bastion and sending an explosive shower of stone splinters into the air.

A Kesho Dawa guerrilla screamed as the slab of stone he'd been standing on suddenly cracked and sledded down the side of the building, sending him to oblivion. His body hit the corner of a rampart below and the screaming stopped abruptly.

The smoking rooftop now had two more ragged gaps on the wall, gaps that were quickly filled by rebels who unloaded M-60s, automatic rifles and grenade launchers at the evading chopper.

But then the second aircraft came out of nowhere.

After flying just above the tree line, it popped up for a few seconds and took aim, the door gunner opening up with his 7.62 mm minigun. A half thousand rounds scythed through the air and studded the battered tier of the building. The heavy metal barrage shredded the rebels caught in the open and sprayed their blood in a mist that rained down from the top of the building.

From his vantage point on a densely treed hill to the north, Jean-Claude Baptiste watched the slaughter through his field glasses. "They're killing us!" he shouted to Bolan. "Cutting us to pieces! Your plan has failed."

"The plan didn't fail," Bolan replied, his voice as full of calm as the guerrilla chieftain's was of rage. "Your men panicked and fired before everyone was in position."

It was a mistake, and in the heat of battle there was no way to prevent it, especially with men who were run ragged and hunted most of their waking hours. Now they could either live with that mistake and keep on fighting, or they could die from it by panicking even more and letting the enemy rout them.

Bolan swiveled slowly to his right, balancing the surface-to-air missile launcher on his shoulder as he tracked the Alouette fleeing from its strafing run. Then he pulled the trigger. With the Stinger's infrared guiding system locked onto the chopper, the missile whooshed out of the tube and homed in on the Alouette aircraft.

The chopper was in the middle of a climb when the missile plowed into its tail. Metal sheets blew off like strips of paper in an explosive wind, then the black-tinged ball of fire sank toward the ground.

Three other SAM trails ripped from the forest cover to the east, their missiles scorching the air and bypassing the remaining Alouette.

It looked as if it was getting away.

But then a fourth rocket plumed through the air, flying right into the cabin and bursting the metal bird into a cloud of smoke and fire. The Kesho Dawa guerrillas cheered at the deadly fireworks, their voices echoing from their scattered positions in the woods and the university.

"It's not over yet," Bolan said, looking to the south where an Aérospatiale Puma was coming up on them. The heavy troop transport helicopter was the first to respond to the Alouettes' calls.

Calls that suddenly went dead.

But there would be other Pumas arriving soon.

"Let's go," Bolan said. "Here comes my ride." They headed down into the woods to welcome the air mobile strike force.

THE FOUR-BLADED main rotor of the Puma drummed the air loudly as the troop carrier homed in on the university ruins. It turned sharply, then circled the edge of the complex and headed toward one of the most suitable landing zones, a patch of tall grass a quarter mile north of the complex.

With the wreckage of the two Alouettes serving as a grim reminder of the rebels below, the Puma gave a wide berth to the vine-covered buildings. Though it kept to the trees, now and then it shot up like a periscope and raked the forest with the minigun.

To the broad-shouldered, broad-bellied Rhodesian merc behind the gun, every burst he fired was an anthem to his old homeland. Like many of the other Rhodies in the FTL, in his mind Zimbabwe didn't exist. It was just a temporary aberration until the white exiles regained power and called them back to duty. But until then it was up to him and the others to stay on the battlefields and stay sharp.

Along with several other contract mercenaries, mostly Rhodesians and Belgians, he stayed sharp by flying in the eagle patrols formed from elite FTL troopers.

The door gunner's heart skipped a few beats as the Puma approached the landing zone again. The downwash plowed a furrow in the treetops, wind and clutter kicking up into the slung-back doors on both sides of the aircraft.

He gripped the handles of the minigun and tracked the forest below. Then he opened up, the 7.62 mm loads spitting thunder and lightning into the woods. The bright flashes and ear-shattering beat of the minigun punctuated the drone of the turbine engines.

Weapons in hand, rucksacks at the ready, the FTL commandos prepared to drop onto the ground and secure the LZ as soon as the Puma landed.

Setting down the massive Puma was always the toughest part.

The LZ had to be large enough to accommodate the fifty-foot main rotors and, when it was weighted down with a full troop load, the helicopter needed to make an angled approach into the zone rather than just drop straight down.

That meant there were only a few places within striking distance of the ruins where they could land if they still wanted to make contact with the guerrillas. The campus was out, because that would be like landing in the middle of a hornet's nest. It had to be one of the few suitable clearings to the north of the complex.

Landing gear extended, the Puma dropped earthward with its elite cargo. On touchdown the light machine gunners jumped out the doors on both sides, each of them triggering bursts as they fell into the grass.

A stream of FTL troops deplaned next, tossing their rucksacks into the grass, then pouring through the open doors like ants ready to go to war. As they dropped prone to the ground, they triggered their AK-47s and formed a circular defense zone around the helicopter.

With the minigun roaring, the light machine gunners sweeping the tree line and the troopers squeezing off controlled bursts, the FTL patrol laid down a steady barrage of automatic fire on all sides. After what had happened to the first patrol, they were figuring that a heavy concentration of rebels were in the area and wasted no time in trying to secure the zone. The steady chatter of weapons howled into the woods, slicing through branches and leaves.

A deafening silence followed the deadly barrage. Then the rebels had their turn.

The Kesho Dawa troops had waited until most of the patrol had deplaned before they opened up from behind the trees, rocks and inclines they'd used for cover. Full-auto fire, smoke grenades and the hellish war cries of the guerrillas roared from the forest. Fire from three different directions took out the door gunner, ripping into his stomach, chest and head. His hands still gripped the minigun as he fell, making the barrel shoot up into the sky. Another man rushed to take his place—a deadly position full of flying lead that kicked him back into the aircraft and sprawled him on his back.

At the edge of the woods, Bolan squeezed the trigger of the Heckler & Koch sniper rifle, picking off the man he'd pegged as the leader, identified by the headset he wore to communicate with the pilot. The guy fell facefirst into the dust storm swirling around the Puma, communication and his life cut off with a single shot.

Ico tore out from the trees like a spindly wraith in jungle-green camouflage, the AK-47 in his hands spitting flame. Then the rest of the guerrilla force stormed the Puma.

Four guerrillas fell from the return fire, but by then the main assault group had reached the line of defense the FTL troops had erected around the Puma. The FTL troops had been in tight spots before, but not against the Kesho Dawa hard-core, not against men who were ready to die for Jean-Claude Baptiste and all he stood for. Several of the surviving members of the patrol stood and backed up toward the aircraft, only to be cut down by a lead volley just as swiftly as if they'd walked into the rotor blades.

Ico reached the Puma first. He fired a burst into the cabin and hurled himself up through the door. As the long-legged guerrilla rolled into the cabin, an FTL trooper snapped the barrel of his AK-47 toward him. The snap was interrupted by the sound of automatic gunfire.

Bolan had fired two shots into the gunman's head and neck, and the man dropped like a stone, dead. Ico met the Executioner's eyes for a split second and laughed, then he jumped to his feet and stood beside the man he'd been so wary of until that moment.

The Executioner, Ico and half a dozen guerrillas swarmed through the cabin and raced for the cockpit. The copilot met them in the doorway of the cabin. As he began to raise a side arm Bolan jammed the barrel of his Beretta into the guy's breastbone and pulled the trigger. The copilot flew back into the cockpit, his deadweight slamming against the glass.

"No, no," the Tongasan pilot cried, raising his hands. "Don't shoot!"

"All right," the Executioner said, slipping the Beretta back into its harness.

"What do you want?"

Bolan nodded at Ico, who stepped forward and disarmed the pilot, then passed the man's automatic pistol back to one of the other guerrillas.

The pilot looked up at the Executioner, sensing a bargain hovering above him.

"Take me and a few others out of here," Bolan told him, "and you'll live. Try anything and you'll die. We've got a pilot of our own to replace you if we have to."

"Where to?"

"For starters," Bolan said, "just get us the hell out of here."

Outside the helicopter Baptiste had marshaled the Kesho Dawa guerrillas. They mopped up the field, punctuating the air now and then with a single shot, while they plucked weapons and magazines from the fallen troopers.

The pilot, who was in his early twenties and had gone to war mainly from the pilot's seat, looked uneasily toward the grim-faced Bolan, who now sat in the copilot's seat. "How do I know you'll keep your end of the bargain when we land again?"

"I gave you my word," Bolan said. "That's the only currency I've got out here."

The pilot stared hard at the man in black, at the eyes that had seen battle a thousand times before. "I'll take it."

Ico stayed on guard while Bolan headed back into the cabin where Baptiste and the guerrillas were tossing salvageable uniforms they'd removed from the FTL troops into the cabin. They were needed in case Bolan and the others had to pass as FTL when they landed.

The guerrilla chieftain shouted up at Bolan, "Good luck—and good fishing!"

"I'll land him if I can," Bolan said, thinking of Wadante trolling his way through England in search of more Acid Bath subjects. "Now clear out. I'll be back."

Baptiste nodded. "I believe you will, Blanski." He waved, then led his men away from the aircraft, the slain guerrillas carried over their shoulders as they headed back into the jungle.

Rather than risk having all of them shot down in the Puma, they'd agreed beforehand that Bolan and a handful of guerrillas would take to the air. Ico would get him to Lake Victoria before he and the other Kesho Dawa guerrillas took to the jungle again.

Bolan would cross Lake Victoria to Kenya. Once there he would head for London and then start looking for Wadante and his school of barracudas.

But there were a lot of "ifs" facing him—if the Puma got away safely, if the contacts who were getting him across the lake were trustworthy and if the FTL hadn't sent some kill teams across into Kenya to wait for him.

Back in the cockpit Bolan gave the pilot the thumbs-up. "All right, guy, take us out of here and you might double your life expectancy."

"From you I'll be safe," the pilot replied. "But if my people find out what happened, they'll kill me."

"That's why I said 'might.'"

6

Arthur Trent nodded politely at the mass murderer who stood across from him in the Tongasan embassy, imagining how nice it would be to pull out a 9 mm automatic pistol and shoot him in the head. Instead, he found himself saying, "I hope you're enjoying your stay in London, Mr. President."

"It's *almost* satisfactory," Wadante said. "Aside from your government's reluctance to provide sorely needed matériel to Tongasa, I have no major complaints."

Several minor ones, though, Trent thought. President Wadante had complained about listening devices implanted in the newly reopened embassy in the fashionable Mayfair district. Bugs in the flowerpots, bugs in the walls, he'd claimed.

It was all such paranoid rubbish, Trent thought. The *bugs* were embedded in the flagpoles sprinkled throughout the embassy, and several light-operated transmitters the size of postage stamps were also planted among the terraces and outdoor crevices all along the building.

"A drink, Arthur?" Wadante asked. Before Trent could respond, the dictator summoned over a uniformed hostess bearing a tray of drinks.

"I'll have what you're having," Trent replied.

When the hostess proffered the tray, both men selected white wine. The woman didn't take her eyes off Wadante, as if at any moment she expected him to produce a bullwhip. Although she acted like she'd rather sleep on a bed of nails than sleep with Wadante, according to intelligence reports she was his number one mistress.

A lot they could do with that, Trent thought. The hard intelligence they needed wasn't coming in. Thanks to Wadante's chief security adviser, an ex-SAS officer named Graham Montgomery, the Tongasan crew was regularly shaking the British intelligence teams or leading them on wild-goose chases throughout London.

Even though the embassy was well miked, countermeasures could be taken. Every embassy had a "black room" sealed off from the outside where they could speak without worrying about eavesdroppers. So far all of the conversations the bugs picked up had been relatively innocuous.

Even more galling was the fact that Montgomery's lodgings by the Thames were even more secure than most embassies, and Wadante had visited the Temple town house quite often. It was impossible to tell what plots they'd hatched while there.

The thought of Montgomery on the loose troubled him. The man was in charge of one of those "security" outfits that could provide a foreign government with up to five hundred well-trained men at a moment's notice. Most of the time they worked with tacit approval of the British government, providing bodyguards, instructors and, more often than not, shock troops.

Montgomery's outfit had been useful in the beginning, but lately he'd gone out-of-bounds. Too many murders outside the country. Too many intrigues. And now the bastard was operating on his own turf.

Practically immune, too, Trent thought gloomily, while he was with Wadante.

"Am I boring you?" Wadante's gruff voice broke into his reverie. In Tongasa those very same words would amount to a death sentence.

"Yes, Mr. President," Trent admitted. "You are."

The man's eyes flared. He stepped back and looked around to see if anyone had heard the insult, and to see if one of his hatchet men was available.

But then the stocky Briton smiled. "All this talk of trade is important, Mr. President, but it's also quite boring. I'd much rather hear about your exploits in the home country. I would be remiss in my duties if I passed up the chance to learn firsthand how you won the hearts of your countrymen."

Wadante smiled. "You play a dangerous game, unlike most of the bureaucrats I've encountered. Perhaps you're more than just the trade official you claim to be."

"Just what you see before you, Mr. President," he said.

Wadante nodded and studied the man. Trent resembled a successful barkeeper as well as a trade official. A stocky man of good humor, his bulk had shifted downward while he'd drifted toward middle age. Now wider at the waist than the chest, he still held reserves of power. But he was no longer a long-distance runner. These days he was a walker, and he still had the habit of walking right into the fire.

Trent had spent much of his career attached to the Ministry of Defense, and though he was officially a trade representative, he was also the ministry's point man for the masked warfare practiced by and against men like Wadante.

It galled him that he couldn't move directly against Wadante. But since the British government still recognized President Wadante as the legitimate head of Tongasa, Trent had to play the part of an official handling the trade difficulties caused by the man's purge of the country.

But even so, at this very moment there was another kind of trade in the works. Though Trent couldn't move against Wadante himself, he could make it easy for someone else to do so. Someone he could trade information and intelligence with.

Just as Trent was the point man for the British government, there was another man working for the Americans—Hal Brognola. With U.S. and U.K. intelligence operations so closely linked, Trent had worked with Brognola in the past to keep their operatives from stepping on one another's toes.

Brognola had informed him that an operation was in the works against Wadante—if Brognola's operative could get out of Tongasa.

Until then Trent was doing whatever he could to tie up Wadante with both official and informal meetings that would go nowhere. The more time he spent with Wadante, the less time the genocidal madman had for drumming up business with his terrorist clients.

Meanwhile, the U.K. services were laying the groundwork for the American operation. It was very hush-hush and only a few with the need to know had been informed of it. Men like Arthur Trent.

Trent could open doors for the American. Then it was up to the American to close them. If something happened that exposed the operation to the public, the British government would deny all connections and the American would have to take whatever came his way alone.

But according to Brognola, his man could handle it. Indeed, he was used to it.

Trent permitted himself a slight smile while the man across from him recounted his great adventures in Tongasa. Wadante spoke like a man who had memorized a fable word for word as he described his rise to power. "And now," Wadante said, "I am backed by everyone in my country."

"Except for the rebels," Trent murmured, sipping his wine and, over the rim of his glass, studying the visage of the enraged Tongasan.

"What do you know of them?"

"Just what I read in the papers and hear on the radio. Things such as how the KDs are gaining support in the hinterlands."

"All lies!" Wadante shouted. "That is the work of conspirators in the Western-controlled media!"

Beautifully coiffed heads turned Wadante's way as debutantes and gray-haired diplomats alike mentally tsk-tsked the man's display of poor manners.

"Well, then," Trent said, "I guess we'll all have to get used to the torrent of lies coming out of Tongasa these days."

Wadante, who had been schooled in appearing as a rational statesman rather than a hot-tempered bandit chief, forced himself to assume a mask of calm. "Yes, well, one must not believe what one hears."

"I understand. Oh, by the way, where is our Graham Montgomery? I was hoping to talk to him."

"*My* Montgomery," Wadante corrected him, "is feeling rather poorly today and has retired to one of the rooms upstairs."

"That's odd," Trent said. "An acquaintance of mine told me he saw him on the streets just a short time ago."

"Your acquaintance was mistaken," Wadante said. "Mr. Montgomery is upstairs. Recuperating."

"I understand."

THE TWO MEN WALKED UP Wardour Street with predatory grace, blending in easily with London's successful film and television crowd.

Producers, directors, researchers, deal makers and actors moved about busily, carrying their dreams on videotape and scripts. Just south of Soho, the district had become a mecca for entertainment professionals.

Both men looked the part.

Graham Montgomery swung his attaché case in an easy pendulum motion as he walked up the street. Dressed in staid dark blue pinstripes and a sedate hat, he could pass as a money man, perhaps a producer.

The American walking next to him, Kyle Vincent, was dressed a bit more relaxed in a light jacket, no tie and a brown cap. A camera with a comfortably faded leather strap was slung over his shoulder. He looked as if he could have been on his way to a commercial shoot.

But the two men had an entirely different kind of shoot in mind.

It was three o'clock in the afternoon, a good time to get lost in the crowds. Not that they expected to be shadowed.

The former SAS man had taken strict measures to shake surveillance, leaving the Tongasan embassy earlier in the day via the back entrance under a canopied carport—at the same time as three other cars had left. They'd driven south to Richmond Park, rendezvoused with some of his security people and then changed cars several times before returning to London and taking further precautions.

Now they were in the clear.

They moved north up to Soho where the storefronts changed right along with the clientele. Neon and nylons dominated. Though the area was still connected to the entertainment business, it was a much seedier kind.

Self-styled studios proliferated, often nothing more than spare storerooms with cheap backdrops that served as sets for cheaply made X-rated videos. The bars and clubs looked dingy in the daylight, rabbit warrens for tired prostitutes. But no one was there for the ambience.

Side by side with the studios were modeling agencies with glossy photos plastered all over the windows. Business cards bearing names such as Mona, Dominique and Lana were taped to the inside of the windows, one on top of the other, like road maps to ecstasy.

They were models who were rented out to "amateur photographers" by the hour or the day. It was a take-out service, with the models bringing the customers back to their hotel rooms. Or for another price, the modeling studio would rent out one of their studio rooms on the premises.

Vincent stopped in front of a rundown model agency with a cracked storefront window. "Paradise awaits," he drawled, pushing open the door that had Paradise Modeling Agency stenciled on the frosted glass.

A jingling of bells clacking against the glass door announced their presence. A thick-chested man with little hair and even less patience jumped up from the sofa and barred their path.

"You must be Saint Peter," Montgomery said, brushing past him while Vincent positioned himself between the hardman and the ex-SAS officer.

At the end of the room a man in rolled-up shirt sleeves sat behind a desk enveloped by stale smoke. Most of his hair was plastered down on his head but a long shining lock hung down over his forehead as stiff as a parrot's beak.

Montgomery nodded. "You must be the chief executive officer of the Paradise Agency."

"That's right," the man said, chasing his words with smoke. "The name's Wes Turner. You the gents who called?" He was slender and looked as if he were on the same diet of heroin he kept his string of girls on.

Exactly the kind of woman they wanted.

"Yes. Where's Lilith?"

"Oh, she's around," the man replied vaguely, making no move to get up from behind the desk. He gestured toward one of the chairs in front of him.

Montgomery dropped into the chair on his right, took out his wallet and passed several notes to the low-rent impresario, who was charging double the fee for the special arrangements requested over the phone.

The man nodded, then pressed the intercom on his desk. "Send Lilith out."

A moment later there was a buzz, and a heavily reinforced door at the end of a corridor opened. A long-legged, dark-eyed woman sauntered into the room, wearing a low-cut summer dress. Despite her obvious charms there was a haunted look about her, as if she'd just come back to the land of the living for this special occasion. Vincent had spotted her during a previous troll through the red light zone.

"Lilith," Montgomery said, reaching out for her hand. "How charming you look."

She nodded and stood beside him.

Then Turner laid down the rules. "All right, gents, it's like this. Wilf—" he nodded toward the hardman. "—goes with you to her place on these kind of sessions." *These kind* obviously meant that he didn't trust either of them. "He makes sure she gets there, and he makes sure she gets back. He waits outside and calls me on the phone if anything doesn't seem right. We take right good care of our girls."

"You're a real prince," Vincent told him.

Turner puffed out another cloud of smoke, then pierced it with his cigarette. "That's what they tell me. Have fun, kids."

The strange parade stepped outside. They climbed into Wilf's Mercedes, a plush number complete with car phone, and drove the few blocks to the walk-up flat where Lilith lived.

Montgomery hustled the woman up the outside staircase, her high heels clicking dully on the splintery, rickety steps. Vincent walked slowly behind them, still on the ground, looking around to see if they had been followed by anyone.

They had. By Wilf.

Turner's henchman had left his watching post at the parked car and was halfway down the alley when Vincent blocked his way. "You can stay down here," he growled.

"I'll wait outside the door."

"No. You'll wait inside the car. This is private business." He spoke pleasantly, still playing with the man. "Just relax. We'll take our pix and then go home."

"You're no photographer," Wilf said, starting to walk by him.

"On the contrary. I'm a good man with a camera."

Vincent shifted his shoulder so that the camera strap slid down his arm and fell into his beefy hand. He swung the heavy camera case and smashed it into Wilf's face with a loud whap. Though he fended off most of the blow, a large red imprint blossomed on the man's right cheek as he staggered backward.

Vincent stepped closer, preparing himself for another strike with the heavily weighted camera case. "Told you I was good," he said. "Want to try another pose?"

But Wilf knew when he was outmanned. If he made a move, he'd end up in the gutter. The guy was a professional. His instinct for self-preservation told him that. At his best Wilf was an amateur. His size made him good for scaring off an overzealous patron or two, but not a man like this.

"All right," Wilf snarled, "I'll be in the car."

"And we'll be up there," Vincent said, dangling the camera like a freshly caught fish. "Practicing our art."

"IT ISN'T DOING ME," Lilith complained. "It isn't grade stuff, is it?"

The needle had been given to the woman a half hour ago, an unexpected bonus, but she was still waiting for the bliss to come.

"It comes on slow," Montgomery told her. "It's a special blend. Just wait. You'll see."

Lilith had been very persistent about finding out the name for what they told her was smack. That was always important to the hitters. White Horse. China White. Afghan Blanket. They wanted to know what kind of bang they were getting. She'd kept on asking for the name until Vincent had shouted angrily from his position at the kitchen table. "We call it Lights Out," he'd said. Then he went back to poring over a week's worth of coffee-stained tabloid newspapers.

"Lights what?" she'd asked.

But he hadn't repeated it, and she stopped asking. She was in a bit of a fog.

Still, it wasn't all that bad. Neither one of them seemed to be violent.

Montgomery was sitting on the daybed, still in its couch incarnation. His suit jacket was slung over the back of one of the wooden chairs in the kitchen. But that was all that he'd removed. He had no intention of testing out the bed with her.

The men chatted easily, but as he spoke Lilith got the feeling he was guiding the conversation for reasons known only to himself. His string of questions took her down paths she didn't want to go—took her walking through neighborhoods she'd thought she'd abandoned back in her teenage years. But those horrible places weren't vacant. A part of her still lived there, still felt it all—the drunkenness, the beatings, the gang boys.

All her friends on the dole, nothing to do day or night but get crazy. That craziness haunted the crowded mews of her youth, narrow, festering corridors she was walking down once more.

It all came back. She found herself revealing everything the man asked. Talking about things she didn't even know.

He was very good at questioning, although now and then the American prompted him with a few questions, steering her back to the same location—her East End childhood, her escape into the music scene as a would-be singer. But she didn't make it. She was just another "almost-was" drifting from pad to pad, trading sexual favors for room and board and not really noticing that each place seemed worse than the one before. And before long she went into it full-time.

She ended up as one of Turner's girls. The Prime Minister of Porn as he liked to call himself.

As she responded to the questioning a flood of names came out. People she hadn't thought of in years walked through her thoughts as if they were in the room with her. Conversations she had had with them years ago suddenly bobbed to the surface, word for word.

Lilith talked quickly, as if she'd had a dose of meth instead of smack. She talked urgently, worried that something would happen if she stopped, that she'd forget what she was talking about. She got the idea that this was some kind of test and her interrogator was seeing how she would respond.

He spoke gently to her. She kept on leaning on him, giggling, grabbing at him, letting him know she was primed to go. But he just kept on with the questions. He didn't want to have sex with her. He really just wanted to talk.

She felt uneasy in his presence, but that wasn't unusual. It happened with most of her customers. A good number of them were just looking for kicks, but there were always the ones who had loose screws and warped fantasies in which she had a leading role.

These two looked almost normal.

The American sat at the table looking bored. He'd made himself at home as if he'd lived here all his life, tilting back his chair, reading one of the newspapers. Every now and then he looked at his watch as if he were waiting for something to happen.

Funny how they worked it. The American gave her the needle. The gentleman gave her the endless quiz.

Couple of freaks, she thought. Couple of heavies.

She could tell by the contents of the briefcase. Though she'd only had a glance when the man with the questions opened it, she'd seen a rack of vials strapped to the inside of the lid. Needles. Gadgets. A long-barreled gun, the kind that serious men used.

They weren't just regular customers. A part of her knew that, and that was why she was glad Wilf was outside. Whenever Turner had an idea the customers might try out some rough stuff, he sent Wilf out as a guardian angel.

Thank God, she thought.

Then her mind froze.

Thank God for what?

She couldn't remember what she'd been thinking about only a moment ago. And then, like rusted train wheels starting up a track, she found her mind working again. But only when the questioner spoke, only when he demanded more answers from her.

"Something's wrong," she said. "I...feel...I feel like I'm floating...like I'm going someplace where I shouldn't."

"So far so good," the American said.

"Don't worry, darling," the questioner soothed. "You'll forget about it soon enough."

The man at the table barked out a sharp laugh, but it seemed so far away, so long ago, that the fear it inspired flickered away like a nightmare breaking. She was glad it was over.

And she was glad the other man was still talking to her. It gave her an anchor to hold on to.

VINCENT RAPPED the window on the driver's side with his knuckles, jarring Wilf from the half trance he'd fallen into. "Roll down the window."

Wilf complied. "What's the matter?"

"There's been a problem. Something's wrong with the girl. You'd better come up and take a look."

"What happened?"

"She's gone blank on us," the American said.

"Come on, man, gone blank my ass. What've you done to her?"

"Like I said. She's gone blank."

Wilf looked up into the American's eyes and tried to decipher what was going on. Neither one of them looked like pain freaks, but you never could tell. Did they damage Lilith? Did she OD? He couldn't read the man, though. The guy was too used to running games on people.

"I'll call in—"

The American's hand shot through the open window and grabbed Wilf's wrist before it could reach the car phone. At the same time he planted his elbow against the hardman's chest and pinned him to the seat.

"I've got to call Turner."

"I know. Just tell him to come here and see for himself. Don't say anything else."

"Or?"

"Or you'll see my mean side."

He made the call and then followed the American back up to Lilith's place.

WES TURNER REACHED for the door only to find it swinging inward. He tumbled off balance into Lilith's flat, heard the door shut behind him, then found himself flung into the middle of the room by a deceptively strong hand. Montgomery's grip was impossible to break. The man's hand was coiled around his wrist as if it were a solid metal band.

Then, in a matter of seconds, his fear-heightened senses figured out what was going on. The stocky American was sitting at the table, a syringe in his hand. Wilf was lying facedown on the floor with a black wound at the back of his skull and a fresh halo of blood surrounding his head.

Lilith sat on the daybed. She was staring off into space, her vacant eyes encased in a pretty shell of mindless flesh. Her lips were moving, but no sounds came out of her mouth.

And the silencer pressed into the back of his neck was no doubt the same one that had been used to put Wilf down for good.

The man's death saddened him. Not because Wilf had worked with him for years—but because Turner might be next. The fact that they hadn't killed him yet made it possible that a deal could still be made.

"Come on, then," Turner said, forcing bravado he didn't feel into his voice. "What do you want? What happened?"

"Ask the good doctor," Montgomery suggested. He pressed the silencer into the back of Turner's head and walked him over to the table where Vincent waited. Thumb resting delicately on the plunger, he held up a hypodermic syringe containing a chalk-colored fluid.

"We fucked up the dosage," he explained. In a conversational tone, as if they were old friends or at least colleagues, he said, "You see, it's a new mix, and unless we find out the exact dosage to use, then our subject switches off too fast."

"I don't get it," Turner said.

"You will." Vincent grabbed the man's arm and rolled up his sleeve.

Turner balked at first, but the pressure of the silencer bowed his head forward. He watched as the needle approached his skin.

"It's all a matter of quality control," Vincent went on. "Before we give this to our...clients, we have to test it out until we get just the right mix." Then he looked up into the porn king's eyes and said, "Trust me."

7

The one-masted dhow knifed through the midnight waters of Lake Victoria. Aside from the restless engine, the craft looked much like its ancestors of the past two thousand years. With its wide but shallow hull it had plenty of room for cargo, whether contraband goods or clandestine travelers like the man in black who sat outside the small makeshift cabin in the stern.

The man hadn't slept or spoken much. Most of the time he just sat by his gear, a bulky black waterproof satchel, watching and waiting patiently for the crossing to be completed.

The crew, a rough-hewn trio from Kenya who might have amused themselves at other times by terrorizing their passenger, stayed away from him for most of the journey. The big man with the graveyard eyes inspired a certain brand of fear of his own.

The captain, Michael Ngombe, had cautioned his crew about their six-foot-plus passenger. "We're carrying a jaguar tonight," he'd said. "Don't make any problems for him. Or for me."

Ngombe had carried everything from fish to fruit to outlawed tusks in his lengthy career as a boatman and had readily agreed to the assignment. He'd been paid well to ferry the man across Lake Victoria to his native Kenya.

It would have been a lot cheaper for the man to book passage on one of the steamships that made continuous circuits of the lake. But it also would have been deadlier.

Many eyes were searching for the "jaguar," and many men were shielding him.

Ngombe had no doubt that the man who'd arranged the nighttime crossing was one of Jean-Claude Baptiste's men. The tall, thin man had promised he'd come back a dozen lifetimes to haunt him if anything happened to the passenger.

Ngombe believed the Tongasan. There was a certain type of magic that could be sensed in a man. The tall man had it. So did the passenger.

And, in a way, so did Michael Ngombe. He had traveled the lake for years. He had friends and enemies on all sides and balanced them well against one another.

He survived. He prospered. And considering the dangers waiting ashore on the countries bordering the lake, that was magic enough for any man.

A light rain fell upon the boat, enveloping it in a cool mist as it cruised into Kenyan waters. The mist was a welcome reprieve from the sweltering rain forest they'd just left behind. When they were about half a mile offshore of Kenya, Ngombe alerted his passenger to their imminent arrival.

A number of trading towns and fishing villages dotted the shore, the lights from their fading campfires shimmering in the night. To the north flickered the lights of the port of Kisumu, their reflections lancing out into the dark waters of the lake.

Ngombe piloted the boat close to the land, the craft skirting the fingers of a rocky spit reaching out from the shore, then rode gently past the inlets that splintered the banks.

Even with his mysterious passenger it was an unremarkable trip, Ngombe thought—until they neared the harbor at Kisumu.

Shadowy figures crept along the waterfront—too many dockhands for this time of night. They flashed searchlights over incoming boats, looking for a special catch.

The searchlights swept out into the lake, seeming almost physical, like bright yellow daggers that pierced his heart.

It was finally happening to him. The odds had caught up to Michael Ngombe. He was at a loss, both for himself and for his cargo. He'd sworn to his passenger that there would be no trouble, that he'd bring him right into the port. But now as he heard voices carrying over the water, voices announcing the arrival of Ngombe's dhow, a spear of fright shot up his spine.

He turned back toward his passenger.

And then a flood of sweet relief washed over him. The black-clad phantom had long since gone over the side.

THE GATES LEAR JET 55 Longhorn cruised at five hundred miles per hour, thirty-five thousand feet above the Kenyan landscape. Flying out of Nairobi's Jomo Kenyatta International Airport, the London-bound jet was an airborne command post. Its computer-laden cockpit and similarly equipped cabin could put it in touch with Washington, D.C., at the drop of a flag.

Though the stand-up headroom in the cabin could accommodate up to ten diplomats for unofficial talks or an equal number of paratroopers for unofficial drops, at the moment there were only two men in the cabin. They sat across from each other at a round mahogany conference table that was anchored to the gold carpeting.

Hal Brognola looked every inch a businessman as he laid out a stream of manila dossiers on top of the glossy surface. There was little that hinted at the man's long career in law enforcement—other than the steel in his eyes.

The man opposite him also looked like a businessman—one whose business was war. Bolan was dressed in black, the clothing he'd worn on his journey to Kenya.

The morning after crossing the lake the warrior had rendezvoused with an officer in Kenya's paramilitary General Service Unit who served as liaison with U.K.

and U.S. security services. The officer had driven him from Kisumu to Nairobi in record time, bypassing police road checks and delivering Bolan to the airport where Brognola had been waiting.

Now, aboard the jet, the two men had a chance to exchange information. Bolan briefed the big Fed on the situation in Tongasa, detailing the setup of the Acid Bath laboratory, the videotaped "confessions" of various captives, including Leon Drew, and the list of potential Acid Bath targets he'd culled from Stefanie Heidegger.

He also gave a situation report on the Kesho Dawa Movement, which was perilous at best. Without a strong dose of support, it might stop moving altogether.

"We're at war, Striker," Brognola said.

"I've heard, loud and clear." The warrior tapped a scarred furrow of flesh that rode above his left ear like a lead-scorched sideburn, a souvenir from the firefight at the university.

Brognola passed a folder across the table. "While you were in-country, we linked up with our friends in London. They've been keeping an eye on Wadante's people, and what they've seen isn't good."

Bolan leafed through the folder, which contained several photographs of the key men who worked for Graham Montgomery. They were hard-looking professionals, many of them former SAS men. The photos were accompanied by a description of Montgomery's U.K. operation and a report on surveillance attempts directed against it.

"These men have been leading the British on a wild-goose chase from London all the way up to the Lake District," Brognola growled. "Montgomery's placed too many teams in the field for them to be covered at all times. We just don't know who Montgomery's targets are yet."

"It'd be a lot simpler if Whitehall just closed Montgomery down," Bolan said. "Hell, better yet, they could take out Wadante himself. They've got the people for it."

"You know and I know that's not the way it's done," Brognola reminded him. "Sure, the British would like to see Wadante terminated—but not on their turf. Not as long as he's the recognized leader of Tongasa."

"But they could put the pressure on Montgomery for a while."

"Maybe not. Monty's been careful. Nothing criminal as far as we know, and he has too many 'friends in high places' protecting him to be put out of business for too long—especially with Wadante singing his praises."

"Hell of a character reference," Bolan said, shaking his head at the tortured logic of the intelligence community. They knew Wadante was a tyrant. They knew a CIA station chief had been abducted and interrogated to death by Montgomery's team. And yet they were playing by some kind of imaginary rule book. Let the other guy do anything he wants—and don't move against him until he walks in and signs a confession. "So they're going to sit around and wait until the Acid Bath crew saps somebody and hope they catch them in the act.''

"That's their plan," Brognola agreed.

"The hell with their plan."

The Executioner leafed through the dossier one more time, committing the faces to memory. He had a feeling he'd cross paths with some of them soon enough. Then he closed the folder and handed it back to Brognola.

He glanced over some of the other dossiers the big Fed had assembled for him. Then, with weariness catching up, he found himself switching off. He'd been running on empty too long.

But there were still a few more details to straighten out. Like the next target for the Acid Bath team.

Brognola clasped his hands and folded them under his chin, a mattress of knuckles for an exhausted man. He was just as tired as Bolan, worn out from fighting an army of bureaucrats in their Washington and London trenches. "Let's go over the candidates this Heidegger woman came up with," the big Fed suggested, "and see what we can come up with."

"All I could get from her was that Wadante has a personal vendetta against the next target. Though she's really just the chemist for the group, she did hear a lot. She believes the target is in the spook trade and operated in Africa for the British."

"That narrows it down to a few thousand."

"Their code name for him is Mr. Quatermaine," Bolan continued. "Or sometimes they call him the

Great White Hunter. Obviously they fear him or respect him a great deal.''

Brognola snorted. ''If they're going to use Acid Bath on him, I'd say they damn well hate him. Anyway, maybe London can help with the Quatermaine angle.''

''I need all the help I can get. But first I need some sleep.'' Bolan pushed away from the table.

Brognola slid the folders aside and stood, dropping his hand on Bolan's shoulder. ''I'm glad you made it out, guy.''

''Right. That's why you want me to go back in.''

''First chance you get. But one more thing before you nod off. Let me give you two magic words to use if the British don't cooperate.''

''Shoot.''

''Arthur Trent.''

''Who's he?''

''A guy like me,'' Brognola said. ''Sort of like my opposite number in the British Ministry of Defense. If you get resistance anywhere down the line, drop his name, drop his number. He'll either break the ice for you or break some heads.''

''Sounds like my kind of guy.''

HIDDEN GOVERNMENT offices sprawled throughout Whitehall, many of them masked by peculiar sounding names, like the Whitehall Land Conservatory Office, which was housed in a gray stone Gothic building near Westminster.

The building had several below-ground levels dating back to the London blitz when underground war rooms were a necessity. The rooms were still a necessity, but now they were being used to fight underground wars.

As Mack Bolan walked down the harshly lit subterranean corridor, his rubber-soled shoes hardly made a sound, contrasting with the steady clopping noise generated by the spit-and-polish oxfords worn by the man beside him. His shoes produced a galloping echo as the two men rounded one corner after another until finally they headed for a door at the end of a cul-de-sac.

The barrel-chested, walrus-mustached man was a clandestine specialist attached to the Ministry of Defense, and it was obvious that he wished nothing more than to get rid of Bolan. But manners counted a lot, especially since the U.S. bankrolled a good portion of the U.K.'s intelligence budget. It wouldn't be politic to brush off the American without giving him a dog-and-pony show.

"This way, Mr. Blanski," he said, unlocking the door and pushing it inward.

"Thanks, Geoffrey." Bolan's contact on the aboveground floor, a cutout as expected, had led him to this somber man who'd introduced himself as Geoffrey. Just Geoffrey. No last names needed here, old boy.

Bolan stepped into the sparsely furnished room. A long, square table adorned with ashtrays and pipe trays occupied the center of the room. It was a sterile room, meant to be used by people who didn't exist for meetings that never happened.

They sat down at the far end of the table where Geoffrey opened his attaché case and removed several files, arranging them neatly one on top of the other.

The Executioner didn't like working with the spook gentry more than he had to. Above all, he was a military man. But without input from the Britons, he might end up leading another charge of the Light Brigade. After all, this was their territory and he was in the dark.

Ten minutes into the meeting he was still in the dark. Geoffrey's well-rehearsed double-talk obscured the details of MoD surveillance of Wadante's crew and in effect offered nothing of real value.

Bolan raised his hand. "Let's put a stop to this right now."

"I don't follow," Geoffrey replied.

"Follow this," Bolan said, his right hand stabbing the air, index finger pointing right between Geoffrey's eyes. "Stop leading me around in circles. Just give the hard intel I came here for and I'll be on my way."

"This is highly irregular—"

"Not irregular enough, guy." Bolan smacked the folders contemptuously and said, "I'll look through this stuff, but I'm sure you've sanitized it. What I want is the intel you're keeping up here." He tapped the side of his temple. "I'm trying to identify Wadante's next target, and unless you want his blood on your hands, I think you'll help me out.''

"I heard you were rather direct."

"I do what has to be done," Bolan told him. "But I don't waste my time or your time. To show what I'm talking about, I'll tell you everything you need to know about this operation, and then you tell me what I have to know. Simple enough."

Geoffrey nodded. "Very well." He pushed the stack of folders aside and said, "Let's get on with it, then."

Bolan told him the relevant details of his sojourn in Tongasa. He also told him about the man code-named Quatermaine whom the Acid Bath team had apparently targeted. It had to be someone highly placed, someone who could be valuable to them. And, judging from their personal grudge, it had to be someone who was an enemy.

A cold grin appeared on Geoffrey's face. He tugged on the ends of his mustache and said, "Quatermaine, is it?" He paused for a moment, then lowered his voice as if he were letting Bolan in on privileged information. "That would be H. Rider Haggard, of course," he said. "He wrote *She* and *King Solomon's Mines* and several other swashbucklers set in Africa."

"Thanks for the crash course in literature, but we still don't know who we're looking for."

"Your first clue hardly narrows it down," Geoffrey replied. "Many an Englishman's gone to Africa because of Haggard's epics. Fancying themselves overlords, colonial kings, adventurers. But the other name they called him—"

"Great White Hunter."

"Yes, if your informant is correct—we can trust she was telling the truth, can't we?"

"I think she was," Bolan said. "I put a gun to her head at the time so I can't be really sure."

"How very droll."

Bolan shrugged.

"Back to our target. If they called him Great White Hunter, that reduces it even more. A few of our chaps in recent years, men very much like your Hemingway, worked in several of our missions in Africa, men who might be called Great White Hunter and take it as a compliment."

"Whoever he is," Bolan said, "he's on their shopping list. I know Wadante's made it a point of honor to get him, and Montgomery's out for his blood, too. Any ideas who earned the number one spot on their hit parade?"

Geoffrey nodded. "There are a couple who come to mind—no matter how much we'd like to forget them."

Bolan leaned forward, his hands spreading out on the smooth surface of the table. "This guy would have to be carrying around a lot of intelligence, enough skeletons in the closet to make it worth their while to sap him and then sell him."

"Yes, yes, of course. I've got just the man. The code names and the matter of a vendetta make this fellow a prime candidate. Among other things, he was our liaison with the French services in Africa. Fancied himself a Great White Hunter type like your Hemingway. Always a mountain to climb, a cause to fight and enemies to make. He wasn't a well-liked man, even among his own.''

"Does he have any connection to Tongasa?"

"Not directly," Geoffrey said. "But he did pull quite a stunt in a neighboring country—which I'm not at liberty to mention just yet. It involved both Montgomery and Wadante. This was before Wadante seized complete power. Back then he was supporting Marxist revolutionary groups all over the continent in the hope they'd recognize his government when he took control of Tongasa."

"And did they?" Bolan said.

Geoffrey smiled. "Not quite. The Marxists in the neighboring country were divided by backbiting, rivalries and conspiracies thanks to a disinformation campaign this Quatermaine fellow launched."

"What happened?"

"Montgomery was scheduled to go into the country, link up with the Marxists and spearhead the coup. But our man delayed him and went in himself—masquerading as Montgomery—and rendezvoused with the rebels. In short order he cuckolded the leader of the Marxists, drained their funds, sabotaged their weapons and then turned over their names and locations to government security troops. He left the country—and then let Montgomery go in—with every surviving Marxist hunting for him. Monty barely made it out with head attached. The revolution failed, and all of Wadante's money was gone."

The Executioner managed a ghost of a smile. The British services had a lot of one-man armies roaming the globe, men who knew what buttons to push. "This Quatermaine sounds like quite a prize. What do you think would happen if he fell into their hands and got the Acid Bath treatment?"

Geoffrey shook his head. "A lot of hard work would come undone. A lot of people would die. Our man knows French and British assets all over the continent. If they were exposed, some shaky governments might get even shakier. Might even fall."

"Not only would Wadante have vengeance, but he'd also have a lot of intelligence to put on the market."

"I'm afraid so, Mr. Blanski."

Bolan clasped his hands together. "Then it looks like he'll be the first target. Who is he and where can I find him?"

Geoffrey smiled. "That I can't tell you. Leave it to our own people to take precautions."

"You don't understand. You have no choice in the matter."

The MoD man stood. "There we disagree. As this is a matter under our jurisdiction, there's little you can do."

"Actually there's quite a lot. Give Arthur Trent a call and get his opinion."

Geoffrey froze where he stood. "Trent? Where'd you pick that name up?"

"He's a friend of a friend," Bolan said. "Which makes us the best of pals. I thought you knew that, and that was why you've been so damned cooperative. Go ahead. Call him."

A look of confusion crossed the man's face. He'd been instructed to cooperate with the American, but hadn't known just how high up the orders had come from. Now he knew, unless it was a bluff. "Sorry. I don't have the number."

"Try this one." Bolan recited the number Brognola had given him.

Geoffrey looked stricken. "Very well," he said, heading for the door. "We'll see. This should only take a moment."

Several minutes later a very changed man walked back into the room. He looked at Bolan as if expecting a thunderbolt from on high. "He said to give you whatever you asked for. Who the hell are you, old boy?"

"Just another Quatermaine, I guess," Bolan replied, and then listened to the secrets that the magic of Arthur Trent's name had unlocked from the vaults.

"The man you're looking for is Ramsey Gould."

8

A cobblestoned walkway led to the front of the stone-walled farmhouse in Somerset. Just south of Glastonbury Tor in hills supposedly haunted by ghost riders from King Arthur's court, the farmhouse was the country home of Thomas Masters.

It was also the home of Kim Roberts, and the home of Ian Halsey, and of Robert Kent.

They were all one and the same person, the well-established identities that Gould had worn throughout a lengthy career in the secret services—SAS, SIS and MoD. His real name was Ramsey Gould, which most people assumed was a cover name. But Gould was the name on register for owning the farm.

Though there were some sheep in the field, it wasn't a working farm. The small flock was part of his cover. Secret service lamb chops, he thought of them. If he had his way, they'd die of old age.

As the sandy-haired, crew-cutted man walked up the path, he puffed on his briar pipe and exhaled an aromatic stream of blue smoke. It was the closest thing to paradise Gould had ever known. No more endless chasing, no more sparring with the brass in London who always complained about his way of doing things—until they decided they needed him. And despite all the legends of ghosts in this part of Britain, the only spooks he worried about were his superiors in London, who always seemed to haunt his holidays.

Gould had quickly gotten used to the pastoral setting, going out to the country more and more often, leaving London behind. London was simply his forward operating base these days while this was his home.

It made him feel relaxed. Too relaxed at times.

The moment Gould closed the front door behind him, he had an uncanny sensation, a windless breeze chilling the back of his neck. He turned slowly and saw a man in black wrapped in the shadows at the top of the wooden staircase. His eyes made out a silenced automatic just as the barrel sighted on his head. The intruder pulled the trigger.

Gould dropped to the bare wooden floor, his chin thudding on the smooth surface. Splinters of wood fell onto his head from the casing above the doorway where the bullet had entered.

"Hello," the Executioner said softly.

"Who the hell are you?" Gould demanded, propping his chin on his hand and looking up the staircase.

"A friend."

"You've got a hell of a way of showing it."

"It's true. Maybe I'm one of the few real friends you've got left."

"I don't know who you are or what you're trying to do," Gould began angrily, "but you'd better listen to—"

"No," Bolan said, "you listen."

Gould turned his head toward the polished oak dry sink two feet to his left, snug against the hall.

"The shotgun's not there anymore. I looked around before you came home from your walk on Magdalene Street."

The British intelligence man looked surprised that his routine had been known. "At least let me get up."

"No," Bolan replied. "It works just fine with you there and me here. I don't have to worry about your trying anything—and my having to kill you. Which would be ironic, considering that I came here to stop other people from killing you."

Gould nodded and found it too uncomfortable with his chin pressed against the floor. He sat up suddenly and leaned against the closed door. "How about I sit up?" he asked, now that it was a fait accompli.

"Fine."

Gould looked up at the splintered doorway. "I guess I'll have to get that fixed now."

"I'd wait," Bolan suggested. "Might as well do everything all at once."

"What do you mean, 'everything'?"

Bolan moved out from the shadows, sitting a few steps lower so that the man could see his eyes. Even so, Gould was weighing the odds of moving against him.

The Executioner was in better shape. Though Gould had been a soldier for two decades, he was an occasional man, while Bolan was always in the field. The good life was catching up to Gould, especially around the waist. And around the brain. He'd let himself get too soft.

"Sorry about the door, guy," Bolan said. "But I figured that would show you just how easy it would be for them to kill you. And to prove that if *I* could get in here after a quick look around, a team of professionals could certainly do the same after a recon."

"Who would try?"

"Graham Montgomery."

"The bastard," Gould gritted. "We're on home ground here."

"And there's a man named Kyle Vincent."

"He's one of *your* bastards."

"Not mine."

"Maybe not, but he's a Yank just the same. Poking around where he doesn't belong. Last time I looked, mate, this was still England. Not the U.S. of A."

Bolan ignored the dig. "And to complete the terrorist trinity, there's Bernard Wadante."

"I should have killed him when I was in the region," Gould said. "But my orders were to keep hands off. No one thought he'd make it to the top."

"Here's a second chance to help take him down," Bolan offered. "If you go along with my plan."

"Don't have much choice now, do I? Put the gun down and I'll give you my answer."

Bolan nodded. He figured what he'd do in the same situation. The man was a professional. So he had to know that if Bolan wanted to kill him, it would have been over and done with and he'd be fit to fertilize the green pastures outside. He laid the silenced Beretta on the stair behind him where it was still within reach. "That better?"

"It loosens a man's tongue," Gould replied.

Bolan nodded, although he didn't buy it. Gould would have to wonder what kind of game was being played with him and who was making up the rules.

The Briton tilted his head and said, "What do you say we—" In midspeech Gould rocketed up from the floor and dived up the stairs. His arms were outstretched, one reaching for the gun, one trying to stiff-arm Bolan's face and block his vision.

The Executioner pistoned his legs, kicking the man square in the chest, just beneath the breastbone. The kick knocked the wind out of him and stalled his attack. Then Bolan shot his right hand out in a palm heel strike, smacking him in the shoulder. The controlled movement used just enough force to guide the man's backward fall rather than hurt him permanently. Gould backpedaled down the staircase, rocked against the wall, then sank into a sitting position.

It was expected. Instead of giving in completely, he had to make an attempt. Now that it was done, out of his system, he could deal with the situation. "Okay, okay," he managed to say when he caught his breath. "I can see that even without a gun you've got the goods. So talk and I'll listen."

Bolan nodded. "You're about to be the target of an operation conducted by Montgomery, whom you know well, and Vincent, whom you know by reputation. Vincent's a CIA interrogator from way back, currently a free-lance inquisitor for Wadante. You're a lucky man if you met him and got by. He likes his work."

"Why come after me?" Gould queried. "From what I hear, Monty's working the Africa trick again, training troops for that tinhorn dictator."

"First, they don't like you very much for the operation you launched against them a while back. Second, they want some information you have. What you're carrying around inside your head could damage French, British and American operations in Africa. It's worth a fortune to them, and they get it all for the price of a needle."

"I wouldn't talk."

Bolan shrugged. "Everybody talks. You wouldn't if you had a choice, but the Acid Bath treatment leaves you wide open. Once it starts, it keeps on going. The drug opens up all your memory centers. A good psychiatrist can pry out whatever he needs. Then they just keep on pushing buttons, the drug multiplies in effect and soon all that's left is a carcass without a brain."

"Nice scare story," Gould commented. "But, hey, anyone can make that up. My compliments for a brilliantly conceived legend."

"We already know they tested it out on a prostitute and a pimp in Soho. One of your spook brethren gave me the transcripts. They were found wandering in the streets, their brains left behind, ranting and raving about an American and an Englishman with needles.

Investigation of the girl's place found another man there, a supposed witness with a bullet in his head. They figure it was a dry run—and you're next in line for some pretty nasty wet work.''

"Why wasn't I told?"

"You're being told now."

Gould shook his head. "What about the police?"

"No police," Bolan said. "No official government involvement from here on in. I want to take them down and get a lead on their next target. I can't do that with a lot of people looking over my shoulder."

"And you arranged all that?"

"Some friends did."

"Who do you hang around with?" Gould asked. "The prime minister and the queen?"

"Close enough. But look, we don't have much time. Wadante's almost finished with this leg of the trip. Next he'll cozy up to the French for aid. That means you'll probably be hit soon. Sapped and carted away for questioning. You won't be coming back."

"You make quite an impression," Gould said, massaging his breastbone where the kick had caught him. "Hell of it is, I'm starting to believe you."

"If you need any more convincing, there are people in your own government I can put you in contact with."

Gould shrugged. "I'll bet you could, and, yes, I'll check you out. I'd be a fool not to. But I think I'm ready to work with you—whoever you are."

"Like I said, I'm a friend." Bolan reached behind him to the war bag sitting on the landing. Inside were the weapons needed to keep that friendship alive.

THEY CAME AT NIGHT.

One moment the lush Somerset landscape was still and dark. The next moment four vehicles knifed through the murky shadows of the forest-lined road approaching Ramsey Gould's farm. Three carloads of men and one black van made up the clandestine parade. After two days of casing the farm, each driver was familiar with every landmark. Just before rounding the last turn that led up to Gould's place, they turned off their headlights.

The lead car drove a quarter mile past the farm before pulling over to the side of the road and stopping. The assault teams were riding in the second and third cars, which stopped midway along the farm, shielded by the thick trees that formed a windbreak on both sides of the front gate. The van hung back at the turn, poised to come in and take delivery once the dirty work was done.

With the dome lights already turned off inside the assault cars, there was little sign of the armed assault team leaving the vehicles. Just a thickening of shadows as the black-clad gunners poured into the night.

"Let's go, let's go," Simon Ladlow whispered, urging the men on, waving his hand toward the farm. This was his operation, so it was his head on the chopping block.

Montgomery had given him a crew of Belgian mercs whose "vacations" in England happened to coincide with Wadante's visit. Rather than use an all-British crew that could be easily tied to him, Montgomery wanted to risk only a few Britons.

The team filtered through the high grass, then climbed the wooden fence and dashed uphill to the farm. There was a good thirty yards where they could be seen by the house. Not that Simon was worried.

The lights had gone out two hours ago. Their target was a creature of habit and was probably sound asleep. The past two nights it had been lights out at ten.

Good night, Ramsey, he thought. Good night, forever.

They reached the top of the hill, then raced toward the house. Six men in all. Six men in black, like undertakers, and Simon was the funeral director. And though death wouldn't come for Ramsey tonight, Simon Ladlow would be the engineer for the man's eventual death after he was spiked, questioned and hung out to dry.

Too damn bad.

Simon was a former SAS man. He'd gravitated toward Montgomery's outfit as his more aboveground assignments had dropped off. Bit by bit he'd found himself working almost exclusively for Montgomery, becoming one of his tried-and-true men. The SAS motto, Who Dares Wins, no longer applied to Simon. Now it was Anything for a Price.

Ladlow paused at the hill, used hand signals to split up the team—three on the left side of the house, three on the right. Nothing fancy. Just a simple break-and-take.

Simon's team spread out on the right side of the farmhouse with Simon positioning himself below the window at the back. One man took the window by the front, and the third man sidled toward the wrap-around front porch. The second team did the same on the other side, two men positioning themselves by the side windows, and one man moving toward the back door.

There would be no escape, Simon thought as he reached into the pouch he carried with him. He took out a roll of black tape, crisscrossed the strips on the lower windowpane, then broke the glass with his gloved hand. The shards stuck to the tape until he peeled them away. Then he reached his hand inside and opened the window.

It was all very simple. He'd go in and unlock the windows and doors. The team would flood in, get the target, then Simon would radio the van that the package was ready.

He was counting his bonus money already.

But in the back of is mind was the soft-spoken voice of his commander. "Kill him if you must," Montgomery had said. "But it would go better for all of us if you took him alive."

Simon took out his silenced .22 automatic, then climbed headfirst through the window, his eyes adjusting quickly to the moon-splashed interior of the house. There was a desk on the opposite wall, and a thick, round rug in the center of the room. The rest of the room was lost in shadow.

His right hand balanced the .22 on the sill, using his palm to inch forward, while his left hand found purchase on the wall.

Serpentlike, he started to inch down the wall.

9

Mack Bolan erupted from the shadows. He snared the intruder at his most vulnerable moment. Doubled over the windowsill, but still unable to reach the floor, Ladlow was in limbo.

The Executioner pinned the man's gunhand against the wall and twisted it sharply. Using the trapped hand as a lever, he clipped the man on the back of the neck with a palm heel strike, turned it into a collar grab and yanked him straight down to the floor.

The guy's head thumped against the wood, then he groaned and lapsed into unconsciousness. Bolan eased the inert form across the floor, disarmed him and removed the hand-held transceiver he was carrying.

"What now?" Gould asked, materializing beside him.

"We got their inside man," Bolan said. "Now we go to work." One man was down and, as his compact nightscope had shown him when he'd scanned the field, there were five more to go.

He directed Gould toward the other side of the farmhouse with a sweep of the Heckler & Koch MP-5. For close-quarters work the silenced 9 mm submachine gun was one of the best friends a man could have.

Since the assault team couldn't afford to make a lot of noise, there was little fear of a heavy metal attack on the first assault. The silenced pistol had shown they were intent on coming in quiet.

But the soldiers in the house were just as discreet. Gould also carried a silenced subgun, a 9 mm Sterling L34A1, one of the few comforts of home he was never without.

As Gould worked his through the connecting room to the opposite side of the house, Bolan made his move. He walked quietly to the front of the house and stopped a couple of feet away from the side window where another backup man waited.

The Executioner stayed out of sight until he heard Gould opening the rear window on the other side of the house. There was a brief scuffling sound, then quiet.

Two down. Just enough time had passed for the man outside to be wondering if everything was okay. Bolan reassured him by unlocking the window and sliding up the lower pane.

The man looked up, expecting to see the advance man from the team. Instead he saw the Executioner. In that critical moment, almost in slow motion, when everything was made clear by the stout-barreled H&K looking his way, the man was debating whether to aim his weapon at Bolan. A short burst from the subgun punched the gunner to the earth, effectively ending the debate.

Bolan stepped away from the window quickly. Though the flash suppressor had reduced the subgun's fire, he didn't want to get caught looking. He opened the front door a half foot and heard a man say, "What happened? I heard something—"

Bolan stuck out his hand and signaled for the man to come inside. A large black-clad shape moved quickly and stealthily up the porch steps and eased through the door. Still clutching the door, he looked inside the room—and then saw stars.

Bolan's uppercut clacked his teeth together. Then, as the man's head rocketed first up, then back down in a daze, Bolan met him with a back fist between the eyes that put him out.

From the front window on Gould's side came the sounds of a suppressed 9 mm volley as the MoD man opened up on his intruder, who'd been spooked by the sounds of scuffling.

Five down. The back doorknob rattled.

The sixth man had decided enough time had passed and was going to force his way in.

Bolan hurried toward the back of the farmhouse, looked at the doorknob turning violently back and forth and triggered a full-auto burst. The 9 mm slugs slammed into the door, the splintered holes matching the entry wounds that drove the sixth man back. He flipped over the railing and dropped into the grass, where he lay still.

"We got them," Gould crowed. "Every damn one of the bloody bastards."

"The first team, yeah. There's more out there, and my guess is that they'll be coming in pretty quick— even if they don't get the go-ahead signal." He showed him the transmitter. "Let's see what our friend has to say."

Bolan dragged the first intruder, the contact man who'd been relieved of his transceiver, into the kitchen. He groaned with every step. The warrior propped him against the sink, folded his head over and turned on the faucet. The rush of water cascaded over the man's head and into his nose and mouth until he began to cough and splutter. He was finally able to talk.

"What happened?" he gasped.

"You're alive," Bolan growled. "For now. If you want to stay that way, give us your name, then give the all-clear sign to the rest of the team. Give us trouble and you're dead."

"All right," the man said. "You win." Still groggy, he mumbled for a few moments, identified himself as Simon Ladlow, then fell to the floor.

Bolan couldn't tell if it was an act or not. The man had gone face-to-face with an unyielding wooden floor, which was like getting hit with a flattened-out baseball bat. He could be out cold or he could be playing for time.

"Make the call," Bolan said.

The man shook his head. "Right, right. Just give me a minute to get clear."

Bolan helped him to a chair at the kitchen table, let him collect himself, then slid the transceiver across the table in front of him. "That's long enough. I don't want you to make a speech to Parliament. Just give the go-ahead to the rest of your team."

Simon propped his left elbow on the table, rested his forehead in his hand then reached for the transceiver.

"Do it right," Bolan warned.

Simon nodded. He thumbed the transmit button and said, "Henhouse Two, Henhouse Two. Henhouse One is ready to run." Then he put down the transceiver.

Bolan didn't like the connotation. But he'd seen more than one operation where the code words made little sense, or else had their own private meanings between sender and receiver.

"No callback?" the Executioner queried. "That's it?"

Simon nodded.

"We'll see."

Gould pulled the warrior off to the side. "You believe him?"

"I'm not willing to bet my life on it."

"Me, neither," Gould agreed.

Bolan nodded back toward their prisoner. "His, I'll risk."

They moved to the front of the house where Gould secured the other two unconscious raiders with nylon cord and carried them off to the side.

Bolan led Simon into the hallway. "Okay, Ladlow, take center stage."

The wiry Briton stared at the Executioner. "I don't follow."

"Follow orders and you'll be fine," he said. He dragged a hard-backed chair to the center of the hallway and positioned it so that it faced the door. Then he nodded his head at the man. "Take a seat."

"But, but—"

"Nothing to worry about," Bolan interrupted. "You gave the all-clear. They'll come in smelling nothing but roses . . . and we capture them. Operation ended." The Executioner turned to Gould, who was readying more cord. "All right, Ramsey. Fasten his seat belt—just in case he takes a ride into hell."

Gould produced more black cord and quickly wrapped it around Ladlow, fastening him to the chair.

"You don't have to do this," the gunner said. "There's nothing to worry about now that I gave them the all-clear. I don't want anyone else to get hurt." Ladlow's words drifted off as he stared at the closed front door, his long face that of a battered Judas.

Neither Bolan nor Gould paid a bit of attention to him. They just waited for the van that was at the moment backing up the driveway, the tires skidding over the stones, the engine whining as it moved uphill in reverse.

As the vehicle whined up the steep grade, Ladlow shouted and lurched to his left. The chair he was strapped to took flight, then tumbled to the floor. The jolt silenced him, but then like a crab in a trap, he scrambled and kicked across the floor.

"Something wrong, guy?" Bolan asked, moving across the hallway to the right side of the house, out of the line of fire from the front door.

Gould took his position on the left, carrying the Remington shotgun that Bolan had returned to him.

"It's... They'll come in firing to finish off Ramsey and get me out of here."

"That's a surprise," Bolan said, hefting a stun grenade in one hand and the Beretta in his right, the threaded sound suppressor tracking the driver's side window.

He nosed the barrel through the half-opened window, and as the driver stuck his head out of the van for a closer look, Bolan squeezed the trigger. The 9 mm slug knocked the man's head back inside the vehicle. He slumped over the steering wheel, his foot falling awkwardly on the gas pedal.

The van thumped into the bottom steps of the porch, ruining the timing of the gunmen inside. While they were still off balance from the thump they flung open the double doors of the van, ready to hose down the doorway with automatic fire.

The Remington roared like a cannon, spraying the interior of the van. Gould wielded the shotgun with tremendous accuracy. With the metal stock folded he had plenty of room to maneuver, punching 12-gauge loads into the van one after the other.

Bolan tossed the stun grenade into the vehicle at the same time. The blast illuminated the gunners, who stood like eyeless statues in the glare. Temporarily blinded by the flash-bang, stunned by the shotgun attack, they were unable to do anything more than squeeze off a few rounds from their submachine guns.

Bolan opened up with his Heckler & Koch while Gould emptied the Remington. The gunmen in the van dropped lifeless to the floor of the vehicle, their uncontrolled subgun blasts chewing up the front door and the ceiling of the porch as they went down. Echoes of the gun battle drifted over the countryside, then fell silent.

The remaining car took the straightest course out of there, screeching down the road, away from Ramsey's farm. The target had become the hunter.

Gould stepped out onto the porch, his eyes searching for the fleeing car on the main road.

"Let them go for now," Bolan advised. "We've got what we need. A link to Montgomery."

Back inside the farmhouse, Bolan headed straight for the trussed-up Ladlow. He gripped the back of the chair with both hands, and then, grunting, lifted it in the air.

"You've got one minute to convince me you're worth keeping alive," Bolan said.

"Put me down."

Bolan nodded and dropped the chair to the floor. The legs cracked and splintered, spilling the man flat on his back. The leader of the raid sat up.

"Hands on your head," Bolan ordered.

Ladlow complied and said, "So now I'm a POW, am I?"

"We're at war, yeah," the warrior said. "But sometimes you can't take prisoners. You crossed us once. That was to be expected. Try it again and you lose the lottery."

"I want some guarantees."

Bolan looked at the MoD man, whose Remington was trained on the prisoner. "Can you work out a deal for him?"

"The deal is," Ramsey said, "I won't blow his bleedin' head off. That's the deal."

Bolan shrugged. "I think Ladlow here's going to want something more. If he gives us enough leads to Montgomery, he'll be worth it."

"And if he doesn't?"

"The shotgun's still loaded," Bolan pointed out. "Use it anytime you have to."

Ladlow had been following the discussion with the devotion of a condemned man. And it had its effect. "All right," he said. "I'll give him up. Monty'll be coming after me, anyway."

"Good. Start with the next target for your traveling circus," the warrior suggested. "Was it here or in France?"

Ladlow looked surprised. "You seem to know enough about it already."

"Not enough to hang the guy," Bolan said. "That's where you come in."

10

A killer waited for Graham Montgomery in the Languedoc château—a long-distance killer.

Two hundred years ago Pierre Foucault would have been Robespierre's right-hand man, picking out friends and enemies alike for the guillotine. And before their heads dropped to the ground he would have already confiscated their properties.

Today he was a diplomat, a special adviser on African affairs, who was often called upon by the French government to smooth out relations with former colonies.

Today he did most of his killing by telephone. With a few cryptic words he could launch an assassination team in at least six countries at any one time.

But that operation was winding down. With so many amateurs entering the game and working for lower prices, the murder-for-hire ring was no longer a big moneymaker.

Pierre Foucault had had to change with the times. That was why he had become one of the chief architects of the Acid Bath program. Not only had he helped in the planning stages, but he'd helped determine who the most profitable targets were and then lined up customers who promised to buy the intelligence extracted from them.

Foucault should have been in a glorious mood. The midafternoon sunlight streaked through the cathedral windows of his fifteenth-century château, the natural light reflecting brightly on the dark wooden interior. With his windows looking out upon the vineyards and Romanesque ruins of southern France, he was living the life of a twentieth-century baron.

But that baronial life-style in the south of France was threatened by a mercenary firefight in the Somerset region of England.

Things had gone badly over there.

Montgomery was no longer in control. Perhaps, Foucault thought, Montgomery's part of the European operation was out of control for good.

The soft jangling of the ivory-handled telephone reminded him of that. It had been ringing constantly these past few days, since the debacle in England.

The silver-haired baron picked it up on the third ring.

"Monsieur Foucault?" the caller said.

"Yes." Though the caller spoke French, Foucault recognized the Teutonic voice. It was Griest. There was no need for him to identify himself, nor was there any need for him to elaborate. Foucault knew why he had called.

"I have most unfortunate news, Monsieur Foucault. Although the prototype looked promising, we've decided not to order any models at this time.

Rest assured, we'll watch your line closely. If it stabilizes, I'm sure we can negotiate once more."

"Of course," Foucault replied. He hung up the phone in disgust.

The prototype was none other than Leon Drew, the most prominent target of the Acid Bath team. That part of the operation had gone well. The videotaped "confessions" of the CIA chief of station had made a huge splash on the underworld circuit. It was supposed to be the first of many more Western spymasters to come.

At least that was the plan. But all that was in jeopardy now.

The Acid Bath team was supposed to be untraceable and infallible, able to snatch intel officers, diplomats or CEOs upon demand. Then they could loot them of their secrets and sell them to the highest bidders—like the German from the terrorist underground who'd been eager to use the team's services.

Until now.

The British intelligence services had flooded the international media with stories about the bungled hit team, making the men who administered the Acid Bath treatments look like a bunch of amateurs. Dead ones at that. The message was clear. Dealing with the Acid Bath team was hazardous to your health.

Foucault shook his head resignedly. He'd been making calls himself, telling his clients that the "product line" was suspended for a while. It was too risky.

Even the long-standing rivals he'd personally selected as targets had gone to ground, almost as if they'd been warned. Most of them were French officials who'd been nosing around his operations, men who might be able to expose his shady practices in France and in places like the French embassy in Tongasa.

His main target in Tongasa was a so-called cultural affairs attaché named André Montrose, who was the most likely contact man with the Kesho Dawas. Montrose was a cautious man, a hard man to catch sleeping. But if Foucault wanted to come out of this, sooner or later he'd have to put Montrose to sleep.

Foucault spent the afternoon thinking over the most immediate problems that faced him. As the sun gave way to night, he was still sitting at his desk, searching for the best course when a pair of headlights stabbed the darkness. The lights flickered through the trees, then washed over the circular driveway that led to the château.

It was Graham Montgomery, driving down from Paris where President Wadante was acting the part of a statesmen. A few minutes later one of the servants showed the Briton into the shadow-cloaked room.

There were no welcomes, no greetings. Just business.

"It's like a bloody crypt in here," Montgomery remarked. "Lighten it up a bit, will you? We're not dead yet."

Foucault snapped on the desk lamp, throwing a small circle of light upon the desk. He cast a cold eye on the new arrival and said, "You've destroyed us, Montgomery. Now that your abduction team fell apart, there's no point in continuing."

The Briton acted as if he hadn't heard. Instead, he leaned forward and stared hard at the Frenchman. "There's no choice in the matter," he said. Saber-thin, and just as dangerous, Montgomery didn't look troubled at all. "We've all put too much into this to turn back now."

"It might be best to cut our losses."

"No one's in a position to do that," Montgomery said flatly. "All for one and all that."

"Is that a threat?"

Montgomery shrugged. "We can't tolerate anyone walking out on us. Too many reputations could be destroyed, too many operations exposed."

"Such as?"

"Take your pick." The Briton shrugged.

It was no bluff. By necessity Montgomery knew about all the black market operations Foucault had set up and could easily expose him. The name of Pierre Foucault was revered throughout France for his tremendous efforts in setting up an organization to get relief supplies sent to Tongasa for the starving refugees.

The organization delivered them into the hands of President Wadante, all right, but Wadante then sold them on the black market, kicking back half the profits to Foucault.

The Frenchman thought he was being cheated by Wadante but didn't dwell on it too much. After all, he cheated Wadante and Montgomery on the profits made from the trade in illegal ivory. Tusks from FTL poachers ended up in Hong Kong, Taiwan and Tokyo, courtesy of the smuggling network Foucault operated throughout East Africa. It was a risky business, but every million counted these days.

Naturally the Englishman was also familiar with Foucault's other African enterprises. They'd worked on several scams together in the past, recognizing each other as kindred spooks.

It was Foucault who'd sponsored Bernard Wadante's rise in Tongasa, diverting covert funds to the tyrant. It was Foucault who'd ransacked the French embassy's files for the names and hideouts of Wadante's opposition. And it was Foucault who'd lured Leon Drew to a meeting where he was abducted by Montgomery's people.

"Do whatever you think you must," Foucault said. "But we still have to shut down the Acid Bath operation indefinitely."

"Perhaps."

"No perhaps," Foucault told him. "I've already shut it down on my end."

Montgomery moved closer and leaned his elbows on the desk. At the same time he steepled his fingers and rocked them slowly back and forth like a pendulum. Sometimes his finger pointed at Foucault, sometimes at himself. Like a loaded gun.

"That was rash," Montgomery said, but his voice was calm, as if he accepted it. "It could jeopardize our earning power and our credibility."

"Credibility!" Foucault shouted. He reached into a desk drawer and snatched out a copy of the London *Times*. "You call this credible?"

Montgomery studied the newspaper.

African Based Terrorists Attempt Kidnap of Top British Defence Officers read the headline. The article went on to say that the terrorists were killed by British security agents who happened to be in the area.

"That's a laugh," Montgomery snorted. "From what I understand, Simon is alive and well and spilling his guts to anyone who'll listen."

"Read on."

Montgomery nodded and looked at the headline below. Wadante in London. He smiled. "Easy to read between the lines, isn't it? That's their way of telling the world who's behind the attacks." He pushed the newspaper away. "But I've seen similar headlines in the past. They can spill all the ink they want, but it doesn't pin anything on us."

"No," he agreed, "not yet. But it does put us out of business for a while. Until you can clean up the trouble back in Tongasa. No one will want to deal with Wadante until his government is secure."

"We're working on it."

"Not hard enough," Foucault said. "I believe it's a matter of a labor problem. My sources in the government tell me it's an American operative who's putting you out of work. First in Tongasa, then in Europe."

"This 'operative,' we believe, is none other than the Executioner."

"Executioner?" Foucault repeated. He spoke the name as if it were a bad dream, then he looked away for a moment, almost as if he were glimpsing the afterlife. "If it is him, we're in trouble. The man can't be bought. We're in for a hell of a fight."

"There we agree," Montgomery said. "But it's not a death sentence. It's a golden opportunity. The same people afraid to deal with us now will be knocking down our door if we take out the Executioner. And better yet, what if we take him alive? Put him to the acid test."

Foucault smiled. "He'd make our fortune and recoup the losses you've cost us."

The Briton laughed. "It's nothing or everything," he said. "Heaven or hell." His eyes narrowed. "But if I'm to keep the flames away, I'll need your help. If indeed we are facing the Executioner, he'll go back to Tongasa to help finish what he started. That means coordinating matters with the rebels and their sympathizers. We know the Executioner has friends in your embassy there. And to neutralize that we need—"

"Stop," Foucault said. "I know what you're suggesting." He waved his hand in the air, dismissing the argument and his cohort all at once. Wearily he said, "I'll see you in Tongasa."

STEEL GUITARS and drums boomed from the tinny jukebox speaker in the Cheetah Hotel in downtown Tongasa. André Montrose sat at his customary table in the front window of the hotel bar and cracked open a new pack of cards. He shuffled them loudly, creating another kind of music for an appreciative audience of off-duty FTL soldiers.

Shadows from the overhead fan crept slowly over the beer-stained tabletop. The blades struggled like windmills without wind, slowly stirring the smoke and stale air above his head. It did nothing for the humid air that bathed the Tongasan capital.

Montrose was a regular at the Cheetah. So were the soldiers from the nearby barracks, along with a coterie of prostitutes and the few adventurous souls who still dared to walk the streets of Tongasa after dark.

The table quickly filled as a trio of FTL soldiers drifted over, joking easily with Montrose. They knew him as a former soldier whose wound had forced him out of the military and into the diplomatic corps. A cultural attaché who found culture in the hotel bar.

As a former military man, the FTL regulars liked him a good deal. As a regular loser in the poker games, they liked him even better. Montrose made sure they always walked away from the table a winner. But he, too, was a winner. By making sure the drinks flowed freely, he loosened the tongues of the soldiers and steadily added to his store of knowledge about FTL operations.

Over the next two hours the card players changed a number of times, and when the game was over for the night, many a soldier was richer.

Montrose stayed at the table, drinking and laughing with a number of Tongasans who stopped by his table in ones and twos.

One of them was named Ico.

After drinking to Ico's health, André waved his hand over his forehead and wiped the sweat away. "Thank God," he said, leaning over the table. "I hear there'll be some rain tomorrow night."

The tall Tongasan nodded and sipped his drink. "Good. We've been looking forward to it. It's been dry too long around here."

After talking for a few more minutes, Ico left. He had the information he needed. The rain was coming, Montrose had said. That was the sign he and the other Kesho Dawas were waiting for, the sign that help was on the way. It would rain all right. A storm clad in black was coming.

As he turned the corner to the next street, Ico picked up his pace. He moved quickly through the darkened back streets of the capital, unaware that other footsteps softly echoed his. They, too, had been watching Montrose. They, too, were waiting for a sign.

11

A Hercules C-130 droned into Tongasan airspace shortly before midnight, piggybacking onto the flight path of a convoy of British and French cargo planes bringing relief supplies into Tongasa. Ostensibly the supplies would be turned over to Tongasan refugees, although there was little reason to doubt that they would end up in private warehouses commandeered for Wadante's cronies.

Still, it helped the two countries maintain a presence in Tongasa until the hoped-for day when Wadante would fall. In the meantime it was a convenient form of diplomatic blackmail. Wadante had promised to keep the remaining Westerners in Tongasa safe—strongly implying that it was conditional upon cargo planes steadily flying into Tongasa National Airport.

The cargo planes were an expected and welcome presence in the sky. But the C-130 was welcomed by another faction entirely—the Kesho Dawa guerrillas. For them it carried a different kind of cargo—crates of Stingers, machine guns, mortars, mines, light antitank weapons, plastic explosives and rations.

The first stage of the airdrop began as the C-130 neared the university ruins that marked the drop zone. Like manna from heaven, the crates were dropped from the plane, their static lines tripping the parachutes and floating the desperately needed weaponry down to the ruins.

A large Kesho Dawa contingent had been waiting below to spirit the supplies away. Ever since the defeat of the eagle patrols the FTL had shied away from the area, especially at night. It had become the hunting grounds of the guerrillas.

The second stage of the operation began forty miles to the south, alongside a wide stream where a village was slowly rebuilding itself after having been leveled by Wadante's troops a year ago.

During his earlier tour with the Kesho Dawas, Bolan had reconned the area well when they'd passed through it. The inhabitants of the village were completely allied with the guerrillas, having had more than enough of Wadante's murderous reign. There was enough room for a drop zone between the village and the stream.

The Executioner crouched in the jump door of the C-130 as it approached the village. Wind shrieked in through the opening, its howl muted by the constant drumming of the C-130's engine. The airstream buffeted the warrior as he mentally prepared to hurl himself out of the plane.

He studied the moonlit landscape below, his eyes drawn to the splash of light at the north end of the village. The interlocking headlights from a quartet of jeeps and pickups was the agreed-upon signal.

His face was blacked and his jumpsuit and gear were also night-black. He was ready to go. With his hands on the edge of the doorframe, Bolan tensed his legs, then sprang out into the night, dropping rapidly toward the earth.

The parachute flared open with a satisfying flapping of cloth and halted his descent. Bolan tugged on the risers, guiding his chute toward the light-splashed LZ. Then, as the earth rose up to meet him, he guided the chute beyond the zone.

It was habit that kept him from landing in the light, habit that made him guide the chute toward the jungle.

He landed near the tree line, touching down in bush that snapped and grabbed at him like a crackling net. He freed himself from his harness and rolled into the woods—just as bright rivets of gunfire drilled the night.

The thrashing sounds of his landing had triggered a hellish barrage of automatic fire from the other side of the stream. Two Kesho Dawas on the other side, supposedly securing the area, were cut down by the men who'd silently moved into position.

The ambushers opened up from two different positions across the stream, the slugs ripping through the branches above Bolan's head. Headlights shattered under the metallic onslaught, followed by the sounds of gunfire punching into the frames of the vehicles and then into the more vulnerable frames of the Kesho

Dawa guerrillas who'd formed the waiting party. Shouts of surprise mingled with cries of pain and curses at the men who'd caught them in a cross fire.

Bolan moved into the trees, keeping low to the ground while lead singed the air overhead. He tore off the strip of tape he'd put over the muzzle of his M-16 to keep dirt out during his landing, then headed toward the stream, stopping near the edge of the jungle. He was in a stand of trees that inched toward the stream. There was a good ten yards of open ground between the trees and the stream, and anyone who stepped into that moonlit stretch would attract a hail of gunfire.

The Executioner reached into his pack for his nightscope then peered across the stream into the jungle on the other side. The nightscope images revealed a half-dozen gunmen to Bolan's left and several more scattered off to the right. They were moving from the trees and closer to the stream.

The warrior glanced through the scope once again, getting another fix on the ambushers. It wasn't the most accurate measure in the world, but it would have to do. He aimed at the section where he'd seen the men advancing, and then, moving his barrel from left to right, squeezed off a full-auto burst. He dropped back to the ground, rolled away from his position and rammed home another magazine.

A streak of gunfire whipped into the trees where he'd been positioned a moment before, attracted by the racket of his gunfire. But then the gunmen stopped. They had other worries coming at them. The

Kesho Dawas had sought cover, and, in ones and twos, began to return fire.

The one-sided war didn't last too long. Ico killed the lights on the jeep that hadn't been hit, then climbed into the back and swiveled the twin-mounted machine guns around. He loosed a burst of 7.62 mm hornets across the stream.

The surviving guerrillas followed suit and kept up a steady barrage at the enemy. Tracers thumped into the banks, then moved up and sliced into the trees.

A group of reinforcements raced from the village into the hellzone, taking up positions at the edge of the tree line, lying prone near the jeeps and crawling closer to the stream as they blasted away.

By now the attackers realized they had completely failed in their objective. They'd missed their target, though Bolan knew just how close they'd come. He would have been cut to pieces if he'd touched down in the LZ, just as dead as the guerrillas who'd been mowed down by the opening rounds of the attack.

Bolan scanned the jungle once again and spotted several of the enemy retreating into the trees. He fired several short bursts, then picked up the scope again. Most of them weren't moving anymore.

Then the gunfire died down. An unearthly quiet fell upon the battlefield.

Bolan emerged from the trees as Ico and the other guerrillas gathered by the edge of the stream. A half-dozen guerrillas clambered into two fishing boats, coaxed the small engines to life and headed for the other side while the others covered them.

"Blanski," Ico called. "I'm glad to see you back." His voice was low, and his eyes kept drifting back to the fallen men whose blood was seeping into the ground.

"Hell of a welcome," Bolan said, moving close to the tall guerrilla.

"The weapons?" Ico asked. "Was there a similar welcome?"

"No. They landed on schedule. No problem."

"Good. But here it's clear we've been followed."

"Or penetrated."

Ico's eyes hardened. "No. Look around you. The blood speaks for itself. None of these people would betray us."

A scream penetrated the stillness, echoing from across the water.

"Looks like we'll find out soon enough," Bolan said. On the other side of the canal he saw dark figures moving in the moonlight, carrying their fallen prey from the forest.

Within five minutes the Kesho Dawas had brought back two of the attackers, both of them severely wounded. One was a white mercenary, the other an FTL ranger.

The guerrillas carried the ambushers from the canal and dumped them unceremoniously onto the ground. Blood streamed from a gaping wound in the mercenary's side. Although both men were near death, the ranger had a head start. He was fading quickly, falling in and out of consciousness.

The other man was struggling to talk. He spoke French, talking to no one and everyone. His eyes were unusually clear—as if he were trying to commit his surroundings to memory because soon he'd have to leave them behind.

"Les Affreux," one of the Kesho Dawas spit, scorn in his voice as he dug his foot into the man's side. *"Sita."* He pointed toward the canal, then drew his hand across his own throat.

Bolan understood. There were six more mercs on the other side of the canal—six who wouldn't commit any more horrors upon the native Tongasans.

As the guerrilla brought his foot back for another kick at the fallen merc, Bolan knifed the air with his hand, shaking his head. "No more."

The guerrilla looked at Ico. The tall guerrilla nodded, then turned toward Bolan. "He's yours, Blanski. For now."

Bolan crouched over the mercenary, who looked up at the guerrillas, registering the thirst for blood in their eyes and in their threatening stances. He lifted his hands weakly, the move encompassing the circle of captors and himself. *"Gens de guerre,"* he whispered. Men of war. Then he spoke in English and in Swahili, trying to touch all bases.

The appeal to military brotherhood didn't wash—not as long as he was serving with the mercenaries known as Les Affreux. Their track record for brutality left little room for mercy. Most likely this man had done his share for the mercs, although, Bolan knew, there could be exceptions.

He knelt beside the man and said, "You're not going to make it. This is where it ends."

The man tugged weakly at the shirt pocket on his right side, which was untouched by the blood spilling from his left. Bolan unclasped the brass button on the man's right pocket and removed a worn and crumpled envelope. It was addressed to a woman in Brussels. A wife, or perhaps a mother or daughter. The merc wanted the material forwarded, as if he'd expected there would be no way to send it there himself.

"I'm not a mailman," Bolan said gruffly. He held the envelope in his hand, as if he were weighing it. Naturally the guerrillas would search it for any intel, but as far as sending it to Belgium... "But your family should know of your death."

The man nodded. He was fading. His eyes were moving back and forth, trying to focus on something.

"They say you're one of the 'horrible ones,'" Bolan stated.

The man shook his head. "I traveled with them, yes, and I fought beside them. But not like them. I was a soldier, not a killer."

"If that's true, then you might have a chance to die peacefully," Bolan said. "You must know what these men want to do to you, how much they hate anyone who has anything to do with the horrible ones. They want to mutilate you."

"What do you want?"

Bolan looked hard at him. "I want to know how you got here. Simple enough. You lost this time around. We won. We're all . . . men of war, after all."

The Executioner had to know if there was an informant inside the hierarchy of the Kesho Dawa Movement. If there was, then the entire rebel structure was jeopardized. Safehouses weren't safe, caches weren't secure and the rebels would be looking over their shoulders from here on in. Running scared wasn't the best way to fight a war.

But if this was just a piece of luck on the FTL's part, that somehow they'd chanced onto the right trail, it was only a small setback. It meant the FTL had access to a good tracking team, men who could shadow Ico and those he came into contact with. But they hadn't penetrated the inner circle of Jean-Claude Baptiste.

"Tell us what we need," Bolan said, slapping the envelope against his palm, "and I'll see that this gets sent home."

"I'll stay here?" the man asked.

"You'll remain here," Bolan agreed. "In one piece."

"Okay." And then he spoke about the FTL counterintelligence operation, how the personnel from the French embassy were shadowed, particularly a man named Montrose.

Bolan felt as if he'd been hit with a hammer. André Montrose was the one man in the French embassy he could always count on. "André is known?"

"Suspected," the man replied. He groaned as the pain began to spread through him like a river flooding the cracked and torn tributaries of his body. "We didn't know for sure, but he was seen speaking with the tall one in the hotel...."

The Belgian searched out Ico with his eyes and said, "He and other suspicious ones were followed. Before the tall one made it to the bush, he stopped and spoke with two men in the capital. We followed them, and they took us to the village. We watched and listened and figured something was coming. It was just a hunch."

Bolan glanced up at Ico to see if the merc's account tallied with the guerrilla. Ico nodded.

"How many men did you have with you?" Bolan asked.

"Fifteen," the Belgian replied.

It made sense. A large force coming to the village would have been noticed, and the operation could have been called off. Besides, the trackers had no guarantee they would strike pay dirt this time out. They were but one of several teams trying to get a lead on the guerrillas.

Bolan asked a couple of more questions, then, as the merc requested, helped prop up his head. Then the warrior stood. "He stays here," he said to Ico.

The Tongasan nodded. "For the rest of his life, which won't be all that long." He ordered the rest of the men to let the mercenary die in peace. Then he and Bolan moved off to the side. "I know I wasn't seen once I reached the jungle," Ico said, "but in the city, there are so many places they can hide. I did meet with two of our contacts as he said. They knew about your arrival.''

"Can you trust them?''

"Yes.''

"Where are they now?''

Ico glanced at the ground, then pointed toward the canal where several guerrillas had fallen. "They are with their friends, about to go on a long journey.''

"We're all going to take that road someday.''

"Our fate, perhaps,'' Ico agreed. "But before you or I go there let us go to Baptiste. And then together we will take Wadante down that road.''

12

The East African sun burned down upon the rooftop throne of President Wadante, who sat in the shade of a gold-threaded canopy, refreshing himself from the ice-clinking pitchers of drinks on a table beside him.

The massive teak-trimmed throne was custom-built to accommodate his bulk and to allow him to look down at the world he ruled. Velvet and silk cushions supported his weight. As if there was any doubt to his kingly pretensions, a swirl of mosaic tiles coiled around him, ending at the foot of the throne, a clear message that he was the center of the universe. At least the tawdry one under his rule.

A few other chairs were scattered on carpets facing the throne, but they were functional and unshaded, befitting the mere mortals who sat in them from time to time.

The rooftop of the heavily fortified mansion in the center of the capital also served as a helipad in case Wadante ever had to exercise the executive privilege of fleeing from his subjects in style. A group of armed guards were positioned around the whitewashed roof-tops, alert for anyone who wished to harm the president—which included nearly everyone who wasn't in the FTL or the administrative posts of his government.

Surrounded by iron fencing, the presidential mansion was in striking contrast to the other buildings left in the area. The fashionable colonial houses that once stood near the mansion had been bulldozed, creating walls of rubble near the remaining homes, most of them two- and three-story structures desperately in need of repair.

A quarter mile from the presidential palace was Embassy Row—or Suicide Street as it had been known during the first few weeks of Wadante's rule when many of the embassies were looted, destroyed or commandeered as temporary prisons. The few embassies that now remained had been fortified to protect the structures and their inhabitants against marauding soldiers or rebelling citizens.

Wadante didn't need to be loved. He needed to be feared. However, the fear machinery he'd installed appeared to be malfunctioning, which was the reason why he'd called Montgomery on the carpet.

"You have no more troops fit to track this man," President Wadante shouted, his hands gripping the arms of the throne as if he were ready to hurl himself at the Briton.

"Technically they're your troops," Montgomery replied. "*Your troops* aren't fit to fight against him."

Wadante raised his eyebrows. "But you are their leader, aren't you? Their trainer? Their spirit?"

The lean Briton impatiently pushed off from his chair and paced back and forth. He hated these presidential inquisitions that gave Wadante the chance to play the part of king. And Montgomery was cast as the fool, the much-vaunted military commander bested by a ragtag band of rebels.

"I work with what I have," Montgomery said. "The mercenaries are good for sustained fighting—once we can find the rebels. And the FTL rangers are good trackers, but they've got to get the thirst for blood, the lust for battle before they can give a spirited account of themselves."

Wadante stabbed the air with a fat cigar, waving it like a scepter. "They reflect their commander. Perhaps it's you who has lost the spirit."

"There's another operation in the works," Montgomery told him. "This one will make us or break us. I've been preparing it for months in the event we would need reserves."

Wadante laughed. "There have been too many events already. Everywhere I turn I see dead soldiers. Dead mercenaries. What is this new force you brag about? More elephant soldiers?" Wadante didn't try to hide the mockery in his voice.

"Ivory soldiers," the Briton replied, using the term he preferred for the cross-border raiders. In the past Montgomery had seasoned some of his FTL regulars by taking them on elephant poaching raids into Kenya's national parks. Herds would be isolated and then slaughtered for their tusks. The tusks would then be moved to storage areas until they were picked up by teams from Pierre Foucault's smuggling network.

It was risky work, it was profitable and it brought the FTL rangers into contact with rival poacher gangs and Kenyan wardens.

A perfect breeding ground for ivory soldiers. But it was too little. Until now.

"This one is different," Montgomery said. "A large-scale raid. Definite contact with other gangs—Somalis, Tanzanians, Ugandans—whoever's in the field chasing the tusks. It'll help us forge a good fighting force."

Wadante seemed pleased. "I like it," he said. "Better than the traditional methods. Training's fine, but blood's better."

Montgomery nodded. "Whoever survives the raid will be seconded to the Executioner battalion. A good way to weed out the weak—and recognize the strong."

"And what is their incentive?" Wadante asked.

"Esprit de corps," he said. "From walking through the fire together."

Wadante shook his head.

"And a fortune for every man who comes back alive," Montgomery added. "Their share of the ivory fortune will be delivered to them once they get the Executioner."

"I like it," Wadante said. "But you English have such a way of making everything sound good—until the bodies fall and the spirits come back to haunt me."

It was Montgomery's turn to laugh. "You need a conscience to be haunted. It doesn't apply in your case."

Wadante stared hard at the Briton, but Montgomery wasn't moved by threats, implied or direct. He was moved only when death stared him in the face, not the promise of death that gazed upon him from Wadante.

"You know me well," the Tongasan stated. "Too well sometimes. That can be dangerous."

"We'll part friends," Montgomery said. "Wealthy ones at that."

"If you can rid me of this enemy, of this man who casts his shadow on me in England, in France, in my very own country, who makes me cut my diplomatic trips short, trips that should have elevated me in the eyes of the world . . ."

Montgomery nodded. It had been a fiasco. The Acid Bath teams had come back in defeat, and though he had several operations in the works, most of them depended on traditional military practices. But the man who was working with the rebels wasn't traditional at all. He didn't play by the rules. He made them.

That was evident by the time Montgomery had returned to Tongasa, bearing little more than canceled contracts from their underworld clients—suspended contracts actually. The contracts would be activated again when the Acid Bath teams proved themselves.

Montgomery needed a victory soon, whether it came from his troops or from Pierre Foucault's diplomatic intrigues. Morale was at its lowest since he'd hooked up with Wadante. A group of elite mercenaries and their Tongasan ranger counterparts had been destroyed in a firefight at a secluded village. These were men who the regular soldiers looked up to. If these veteran soldiers were destroyed, what could the regulars hope to accomplish?

By all rights it should have been a victory for Montgomery's men. The strike team had had a chance to capture the Executioner, trailing the guerrillas right to the village where he was parachuting into. Instead, the rangers and mercenaries had been ripped apart, with only a few of them returning alive to tell the story.

An FTL revenge troop had been sent to the village where the firefight had occurred, but by the time they'd gotten there the Tongasans were gone. The entire village had been abandoned.

And though the rebels were gone, they'd left behind a number of improvised booby traps that took out another dozen FTL soldiers. An explosive combination of gasoline and grenades had ignited when the soldiers had begun their customary looting—triggering the traps wired to family heirlooms and supplies.

The FTL troops had returned to their base convinced the war was lost. After all, their numbers had just been decimated by villagers who were no longer there.

There were too many similar instances these days. More and more Tongasans fled the towns and moved into outlying villages where they could support the

Kesho Dawas. Unless the tide was turned, even the FTL regulars would look for another leader. And more and more of them would desert and join the other side.

"I must go," Montgomery said. "If this works well, upon my return I'll have identified the very best, the most ruthless soldiers who serve you."

"And if not?"

Montgomery shrugged. "If not, then at least we'll make a fortune from the tusk trade."

"And then you'll leave?" Wadante queried.

"No," he answered. "I'll leave when I have the Executioner's head in my hand."

THE IVORY-INLAID stock of the AK-47 assault rifle gleamed in the sunlight. Alexander Tenga stepped from the bush and slowly moved through the high grass. There was a full 30-round magazine in the weapon and a thirst in Tenga that could only be slaked by more ivory.

The man wore camouflage fatigues, as did the half-dozen other men who stepped into the grass. They also carried automatic weapons and other tools of the trade. But only Tenga's weapon had the inlaid ivory. It marked him as a veteran of the FTL poaching gangs. A leader.

Now he had to teach the trade to his apprentices.

When the poachers stepped farther into the open, a large bull elephant raised its mammoth head from the water hole where it was satisfying its thirst. The creature looked their way, trumpeted angrily, feinted toward them in a short charge, then abruptly turned back to the water. The other elephants in the herd followed its lead, keeping wary eyes on the intruders, but drinking their fill.

There were several good-sized tusks in the herd. Tenga motioned the men to move forward. At the same moment another FTL gang approached from the opposite end of the clearing.

They'd all made the clandestine crossing into Kenya without any problem, coming into the country aboard fishing boats and passenger ships. Once they'd reached the shore, a ragged fleet of cars had brought them inland. The drivers were well paid to keep their mouths shut and to bring them to their staging points.

Tenga's group in Tsavo National Park was just one of several FTL poaching gangs who'd infiltrated the nearly eight thousand square miles of wilderness.

Just one park among many. Aberdares National Park, about one hundred miles north of Nairobi, was also being stalked for ivory. Masai National Reserve, close to Lake Victoria, had also been targeted, as had Meru National Park in the north.

This was more than just a poaching raid. It was an expedition. Montgomery had brought the gangs over and sprinkled them throughout the parks, salting his veteran raiders among them—each gang needed someone who knew the score.

Kenyan park rangers patrolled the vast wilderness as best they could, and shot at suspected poachers first and asked questions later. They had quick reaction teams and often flew in by helicopter to shoot the hell out of poachers' camps or to drop park rangers to follow their tracks and gun them down.

It was no longer a game to them; it was war.

It was a hunting ground, and it was the perfect training ground for Montgomery's Executioner battalion.

Tenga waved his hand forward, signaling the charge to begin. The poachers streamed through the grass, moving as fast as they could. The elephants noticed them—just as they noticed the other pack of poachers charging from the other side.

The poachers opened up with their weapons, and bursts of gunfire struck the great gray hides, spouts of blood erupting into the air. As the enraged animals roared and staggered, turning about to face their enemies, the AK-47s drilled them head-on.

Deadly projectiles sang through the air in relentless full-auto bursts. The gray beasts shrieked in hideous chorus as they crashed to the earth, rivers of blood staining the grass.

One elephant charged Tenga's group, picking out a poacher who stood frozen in place, panic-stricken, his assault rifle empty. Blood sprayed from the animal's head with every step as the lead fusillade from other poachers ate into it. It managed a last scream as it went down, its tree-stump-sized foot crushing the stunned rifleman's chest to a pulp.

Tenga ignored the man. Except for having the body stripped of all ID after the hunt was over, there was nothing more to do for him. And at the moment there were more important things to do than grieve.

Tenga triggered another burst.

The steady volleys of gunfire took their toll. Soon the only elephants standing were the younger ones who nosed around the groaning and bleeding wrecks on the ground.

Then the hatchet men went to work, their axes slicing through the air and into the carcasses. Next came the whine of chain saws cutting into bone.

Tenga stood to one side as his men gathered up the tusks. Now that the men had whetted their killer appetites on the elephant herds, they were ready for the more dangerous game Montgomery had in mind. It was time to leave the slaughterground and rejoin his leader.

13

The heavily armed gang of Kenyan and Tanzanian poachers moved noisily through the jungle. The two groups had banded together for protection against the increasingly aggressive park rangers.

The poachers had been prowling in Tsavo National Park for several days running, looking for elephant herds. If no elephants were to be found, they intended to go after tourists. Despite a recent spate of murders in the national parks, tourists continued to drive on some of the more remote roads that led into the wilderness so that they could see the sights, get a glimpse of the "real" Africa.

But the poachers had been lucky on this hunt and were carrying with them several recently captured tusks.

The gang cut through the forest and headed for a crystal-clear waterfall. The rush of the cascading water signaled that their expedition would soon be at an end. Just south of the falls their boats were stashed in the thick bush that followed the river.

Only a small clearing separated them from the river. The ivory would be loaded onto the boats and the men would be on their way, leaving Tsavo National Park as rich men.

The leader of the poachers, a quick-witted Tanzanian stopped abruptly in midstride, his eye catching a movement in the trees ahead. It was just a fleeting motion on the periphery of his vision, but it registered nonetheless.

With the finely honed instincts that had kept him alive for more than a decade in the illegal ivory trade, the Tanzanian raised his hand to halt the troops. To a man they dropped into a crouch, scanning the wilderness ahead of them.

Nothing.

After waiting a full two minutes with the sun beating down upon them, the Tanzanian motioned them forward again. He was satisfied it was just nerves. For the past several days he'd been living on the edge, expecting combat at any moment. Now that their mission was complete, his body was catching up to him.

He smiled. Soon he would reap the rewards.

AT MONTGOMERY'S command the First Tongasan Legion stepped out from behind their shelters along the river's edge. With their jungle-camouflage fatigues blending in with the surrounding trees, the FTL soldiers moved practically unseen. But even so there was a slight rustle as they took aim at the oncoming gang.

The Tanzanian-led poachers stopped in their tracks, and for one brief moment they stared down at the small army in their path.

"Fire!" Montgomery shouted.

The FTL gang opened up with everything they had, pelting the tall grass with a storm of lead. The startled poachers fell backward in waves, half of them down and dead within the first seconds of the firefight.

The remaining poachers tried to retreat, but Montgomery sent a dozen FTL rangers, led by Alexander Tenga, to outflank them. While the rest of the FTL pinned the poachers, Tenga's men moved off to the left and double-timed along a ridge that let them cut off the poachers' retreat.

The rest of the FTL men moved out into the field.

The trapped poachers had no choice. Running was suicide. But by staying and fighting they could at least take down some of their attackers.

They rose up like phantoms and fired their automatic rifles wildly. Their leader pivoted around in a half circle, triggering bursts at the FTL soldiers tightening the noose. His men followed his lead.

The last-ditch barrage dropped five FTL raiders to the ground, one of them Alexander Tenga, who caught three rounds in his legs and one in his chest as he fell.

While the poachers scrambled to reload, the FTL charged. Like the elephants they'd slain so carefully before, the trapped poachers were riveted by point-blank bursts of automatic fire.

Clip after clip was emptied into them. Finally the screams stopped and smoke cleared, leaving behind the stink of cordite and blood.

Montgomery dispatched one team to round up the tusks dropped by the poaching gang, and another to search the bodies of the fallen FTL troopers and make sure they left nothing behind to tie them to Tongasa.

"Tenga's still alive," one of the men shouted.

Montgomery nodded. He walked through the tall grass to the spot where Tenga lay bleeding. He was pretty well shot up. The wounds were bad. Not impossible to heal, but bad.

Montgomery shook his head.

"The park rangers will be on our trail soon. Helicopters. Ground teams. The works."

Tenga looked up at him, coughing now, his body shaking with chills beneath the hot African sun. "They'll kill me," he said. "They'll kill me if they find me."

"No they won't."

Tenga's face lit up with hope. Until Montgomery obliterated it with a 3-round blast.

The Briton knelt beside him, almost as if he were going to give him last rites. But then he found what he was looking for, buried in the grass. He picked up the ivory-inlaid AK-47 and walked away from the bodies.

"Hurry up," he shouted over his shoulder. "We've got a lot of ground to cover before we start our next hunt."

The gang of survivors followed him. They were smaller in number than before, but they were a little bit more hardened, a little more bloodthirsty.

They were Montgomery's kind of men.

THE SAND-COLORED JEEP crunched over the barren soil as it raced down the hilly trail. It followed the slanting curve for another half mile before coming to a stop near the stand of scrub trees.

André Montrose climbed down from the vehicle.

He was an hour north of the Tongasan capital. He'd been followed at first, but by driving like a maniac— a reputation he'd earned from the moment he'd first set foot in Tongasa—he'd been able to shake them.

He headed for the trees, cautiously looking around. Footsteps rustled through the grass behind him, and he turned to see Mack Bolan emerging from the scrub on the other side of the trail, submachine gun cradled in his arms.

"Hello, André."

André nodded. "Mack...I was hoping you'd make it."

"Now that's something we finally agree on."

Montrose shrugged. "We saw different sides of the battle before. You in the field. Me in the embassy. We have different strengths, different weaknesses. We couldn't help seeing different ways of moving against Wadante."

"Yeah," Bolan said. "The only way that works against men like Wadante is to come in hard and fast. From start to finish."

Montrose nodded. "I would have liked to urge my people to act sooner, but the embassy's at war with itself these days. Some people sided with us. Others backed Foucault—who's en route even as we speak."

"The thieves are coming home to roost," Bolan said.

"Your European trip worked wonders. Forced them to close down their operation."

"And prepare the inevitable counteroffensive," the warrior replied.

The Frenchman nodded. "From all appearances it's already started. Not here, but in Kenya. We think it's related to a series of attacks in their national parks."

"Seems to be a lot of attacks there," Bolan commented. "Too many tourists and tusks for the bandits to resist."

"It's more than the bandits this time." Montrose briefed Bolan on the large-scale assaults in Kenya. "It's been a regular war over there. Poacher against poacher against park ranger. A lot of casualties. A lot of organization. The feeling in the embassy is that Montgomery's combined his illegal ivory trade with on-the-job training. He's vetting the FTL irregulars. The ones who come back will most likely come after you."

"Just because there's increased activity doesn't mean Montgomery's behind it."

"By itself, no," Montrose agreed. "But the attacks began shortly after Montgomery left Tongasa. Simultaneously a large number of FTL troops were suddenly unaccounted for. The skirmishes had his mark on them. On several occasions the gangs revealed themselves when they could have escaped undetected. It's as if they were spoiling for action. A lot of lives were thrown away, as if Montgomery wanted to get rid of deadweight.''

Bolan listened intently. Montrose's contacts in Kenya had a detailed knowledge of the government's response. Security and police forces had descended upon the parks. There had been a lot of casualties on both sides. The poachers were holding their own.

"Efficient, aren't they?'' the warrior commented. "Foucault comes here to coordinate the smuggling network and at the same time Montgomery raises a task force.''

"Too bad we couldn't strike while they're out of the country.''

Bolan nodded. "It would be suicide now. Baptiste's people are gathering for an all-out assault, but it'll take time for the Kesho Dawas to get themselves and the matériel in place. In the meantime I've got some business of my own in Tongasa. But first, let's pool our intel.''

The Executioner told him of the successful airdrop and the supplies now available to the guerrillas. But they needed to know where to employ it.

That was Montrose's territory. The Frenchman was in charge of the Groupe d'Intervention de la Gendarmerie Nationale contingent that had been attached to the embassy even before Wadante's reign had begun.

Masquerading as a cultural attaché, Montrose had long ago been made as a spook by Wadante's crew.

But they didn't know his background with GIGN. Montrose had been in on the formation of the organization when it was established in the early seventies. In those days he'd worked out of GIGN-4's headquarters at Mont-de-Marsan, responsible for antiterrorist operations in southern France and points farther south.

As an antiterrorist specialist, his role in GIGN had been closely guarded, even from men like Pierre Foucault. A fortunate thing, now that Foucault himself had become a terrorist.

While the *gigenes* had played an important part in training Tongasan police and setting up the security system, it wasn't totally out of the goodness of their hearts. Now they knew where the FTL quick-reaction teams were stationed, the locations of the communications networks, the armories, the troops. They knew emergency evacuation procedures and the routes Wadante's forces would take.

Montrose willingly gave the information to the Executioner.

The two men talked for some time. There was total trust between the two men. Montrose had been Bolan's contact right from the beginning when he'd steered the Executioner toward the prison where Leon Drew was being held. They'd both been fighting wars in their own way. But now that was coming to a head.

With Foucault in-country there would be no more halfway measures. Foucault was an old SDECE man—Service de Documentation Extérier et de Contre-Espionnage—whose ruthless methods made him a standout in that often brutal intelligence service. He wouldn't waste too much time before he moved on Montrose and arranged a fatal accident for him.

"Unless we act soon," Montrose said, "everything we've worked for will be destroyed."

Bolan nodded. "I'll get word to you as soon as they're all in position."

"We'll need every man."

"And woman."

Montrose looked surprised. "Any woman in particular?"

"Yeah. Stefanie Heidegger."

"She's as bad as the rest of them!" Montrose protested.

"Maybe. Maybe not. I've found out a few things that might bring her into our camp. Besides, she and I have a bargain."

Although he looked doubtful, Montrose was still willing to help. "You'd better act fast then," he said. "They're easing her out of the loop now that her value is limited, I'm surprised they've kept her alive this long."

"If she's feeling the heat, then—"

"Then you'll apply the torch," Montrose finished. He filled Bolan in on her whereabouts, her schedule and her fall from grace.

14

Bolan sprinted across the night-darkened Boulevard des Martyrs under a cloud of dust kicked up from the FTL troop transport wheezing down the street. As the vehicle rounded a corner, the Executioner sought out the shadows of the two-story buildings that lined the street.

He concealed himself more out of habit than concern about being seen by locals. They wouldn't be watching. These days it was wiser to look the other way rather than report crime in the streets. Especially since most crime was committed by police or FTL soldiers making their rounds.

Only those willing to risk death walked the streets at night.

The warrior slowly worked his way south toward the park on the south end of the boulevard that at one time had been a popular spot for young lovers to stroll through. But that had stopped when the hangings had begun at the beginning of Wadante's rule. Tongasans suspected of harboring ill feelings against the dictator were dragged from their houses by secret police. They were beaten and hanged, their bloated bodies left dangling from the trees as a lesson for those who would oppose Wadante.

It had been renamed the Boulevard des Martyrs after a group of citizens had cornered one of the police death squads, turned their own weapons on them and exterminated the bloodthirsty lawmen. Wadante's propaganda machine had transformed the police from homicidal goons to patriotic martyrs. They were avenged ten times over in the bloodbath that followed.

Now the Boulevard des Martyrs was quiet. Deserted.

It was a residential area in the center of Tongasa, and Stefanie Heidegger had made her home there.

Bolan finished his recon of the hard sites that André Montrose had pointed out to him, and now he had one more place to visit. Stefanie Heidegger was about to make up her mind once and for all where she stood in the winds of war gusting through the streets of Tongasa.

JACQUES SARAI KNOCKED on the door with the butt of his submachine gun. "Police," he called. "Open up."

Lights flickered out in the neighboring houses.

A door bolt hammered home in the apartment below. He ignored it. He was more interested in the occupant on the second floor of the colonial mansion. The lights stayed on in the flat, but there was no sound.

The bull-necked, uniformed man smiled and tapped the barrel of the subgun against the glass in irritating cadence. "Stefffaneeeeee," he cooed in a singsong voice.

He gouged the barrel back and forth across the glass, like a feral creature scratching to get in, like one of the vampires in the American videotapes he and his subordinates in the Tongasan Security Squad watched.

Splatter movies and pornographic tapes were their main indoctrination into Western culture. They liked what they saw and were eager to duplicate it.

At the moment Jacques was running a private X-rated tape in his mind, starring himself and Stefanie Heidegger.

He shouted her name again, but got no response. He waited and listened, staying silent long enough so that she'd think he'd gone away.

Finally there were tentative sounds coming from inside, footsteps on the carpet. She was moving around, thinking it was all clear.

He rapped on the door.

"Go away!" she shouted. Her voice was loud and frightened, coming from one of the inner rooms of the apartment, as if she were afraid to come too close to the door because he might reach in and grab her.

The rapping continued.

"Do that again and I'll report you to Kyle Vincent," she threatened.

Jacques Sarai laughed. "I'll report myself for you," he said. "Monsieur Vincent dispatched me here himself. I'm your bodyguard now, Stefanie."

The lie still echoing in the darkness, Sarai patrolled the wooden balcony, his steps rumbling over the slats in a maddeningly precise rhythm.

He smiled. The goosestepping cadence added yet another fine touch of terror. Each night he'd grown bolder in his harassment, testing to see if the woman still had any pull left, any protection from the American or British warlords. But there had been no recriminations. Perhaps she had already mentioned the harassment to Vincent and he'd done nothing, or perhaps she was even afraid to bring it up with him in the first place.

Either way it meant one thing. The woman was fair game. She was on the outs with the FTL high command.

But Jacques Sarai was rising steadily.

He was in his late thirties, old age for a man in his line of work. Death squads went in and out of fashion. If you backed the wrong faction, you were permanently out. He knew that from personal experience. He'd sent many an old friend to his grave with a well-placed shot. He liked to do it while they were in the middle of a conversation—making the other man think it was some kind of joke right until the punch line cored a 9 mm hole in his skull.

Finding her voice again, Stefanie cocooned her terror in a shrill demand. "I'll have you shot unless you leave right now!"

Sarai shook his head sadly. The woman would have to be taught not to challenge him. Before the night was over he would share with her some of the skills he'd

learned in the blood-soaked hallways at the secret police headquarters.

"Your position's declining, miss. You are in exile
now. That's why you were sent here. No longer in the
palace. That's why I've been appointed your personal
bodyguard."

"You're lying."

"It's my duty to protect you, whether you want it or
not. Now let me in."

THE REDHEAD CHEMIST was finally waking up from
the dream of revolution that had gradually turned into
a nightmare. It had taken years, but now the veils were
being pulled back. This wasn't the America Stefanie
Heidegger had railed against for so long. Nor was it
the Europe she dismissed as a bourgeois prison. No,
this was Tongasa, the Third World paradise she'd
helped to create.

Acid Bath was the apple.

Kyle Vincent was the serpent.

There was no one to complain to—except herself,
and that part of her mind was no longer listening. Now
the instinct for survival was kicking in. The part of her
mind that shouted out to live no matter what was now
taking control.

The grating of metal on glass sounded once more.
The noise enraged her, but made her shiver at the same
time. She knew it was a calculated maneuver on Sarai's part, but the tactic was effective nonetheless.

She thought of how many other women heard that
same sound during Wadante's reign. *Other women*.

That was the key. It had always been other women. Always someone else suffered. As long as she was a pivotal member of the power structure, she'd been able to look the other way. She'd been able to keep her distance from the madness.

But now it was here in the form of Jacques Sarai.

She wrapped her light satin robe around her, pulling the drawstrings tight. The flimsy garment was enough to protect her from the occasional breeze, but not the gaze of the Tongasan terrorist who'd been haunting her door for the past few nights.

She looked at the phone on the bedside table. No use. It was disconnected. Even if it had been working, there was no one she could call whom she trusted.

The chemist reached into her purse, rummaged through the contents and took out a heavily weighted cartridge pen from the bottom.

"Stefanie," Jacques called, "open the door." His voice was low, threatening, like a storm about to be unleashed. "The game is over."

She bit her lip and turned toward the door. She thought of Kyle Vincent and Graham Montgomery and how quickly either of them could dispatch the thug outside her door. If they wanted to.

But there would be no help from them.

Ever since their return from their European trip, the Acid Bath team had been cold to her, almost as if it were her fault that the Ministry of Culture had been penetrated. She was no longer trusted as she used to be.

Kyle Vincent had taken to hanging around the lab when she was there, constantly asking questions about her work. Too many. Instinct made her hold back on some of the questions and give misleading answers on the others. If Vincent and Montgomery had all the answers, they wouldn't need her.

The masks were coming off.

And soon they would all reveal faces like that of the butcher who stood outside her door.

The latch turned.

A sliver of metal ferreted into the lock, rasping back and forth, tripping the tumblers.

She dropped the cartridge pen into a shallow half pocket on the right side of her robe just as the door swung open and banged against the wall with a thud.

Jacques Sarai filled the doorway, a moonlit hulk searching for his prize. Then he slammed the door shut behind him and locked the bolt in place.

A WOMAN'S SCREAM rippled through the night. Bolan glanced down the street, pinpointing the direction of the sound. Only one light shone from the string of houses.

Stefanie Heidegger's.

The Executioner ran silently through the shadows, emerging beneath a wooden staircase that led to the second floor.

Grabbing the railing as an anchor, he launched himself up the stairs and threw himself against the door, his left hand turning the knob and finding it locked, right shoulder continuing forward, smashing against the wood and shuddering the door free.

As it swung open, he went down, rolled across the floor and came up in a crouch, his right hand clutching the silenced Beretta. The occupants of the room froze in place as if they were held in suspended animation, their heads turned toward the Executioner.

Then, slowly, the strange tableau unfolded. With badge and ribbons hanging from his uniform, Jacques Sarai stood beneath the doorway of Stefanie's bedroom, his hands gripping her shoulders. He stared at Bolan, but not out of fear. Rather it was shock. "You are too late," he said. "The girl is mine. Go back to your quarters."

Bolan hid his surprise. The security man was blind to the enemy that had entered his domain, seeing him only as a competitor poaching on his hunting grounds. It seemed perfectly logical to the Tongasan that a suitor would come calling on Stefanie with gun in hand and rape in mind.

Disheveled and speechless, Stefanie Heidegger glanced first at Bolan, then at the thick-necked security man, her hand dipping into a small pocket of her robe.

The Tongasan stared almost casually at the weapon, having been in many standoffs before. And survived them. "I said you must leave at once," Sarai repeated. "She's mine."

"The girl is no one's," Bolan stated, stepping forward, the silenced Beretta bearing down on the security man like a dowsing rod.

Sarai twisted the fabric on the girl's shoulders, spinning her around to use her as a shield. But the secret policeman still hadn't put together what was happening.

The man the entire FTL was searching for stood just a few yards away from him and all Sarai could think of was the spoils of war.

The policeman's hand fell from Stefanie's shoulder and dropped out of sight. But his shoulder moved slightly. "Back to your barracks," he said. "Les Affreux must go hungry tonight."

"I'm not one of your mercenaries."

"Regardless. The Security Squad has jurisdiction over everyone in Tongasa no matter who you are."

Bolan watched Sarai's almost imperceptible motions as the man prepared to make his move. One quick shot and Bolan could silence him forever. But if he took him alive, he might learn more about the FTL setup in Tongasa.

Sarai took a step backward into the bedroom, pulling his human shield with him. "Do you know who I am?"

"Yeah," Bolan replied. "You're the reason why I'm here. One of thousands."

"What are you talking about?" The question was only a diversion. Even as he spoke Sarai flung Stefanie out of the way and lashed out with his knife hand.

Bolan dropped to the floor flat on his back as the knife hurled overhead. The blade bit into the plaster wall and stuck into the wooden beam behind it.

The Executioner raised his knees just as the uniformed thug dived through the air, a hammer fist aimed at Bolan's temple. But Bolan's knees struck first, slamming into the man's jaw with a loud clack and an explosion of blood. For a moment the Tongasan was suspended there, his bloody mouth gaping.

His maddened eyes, watering from pain and shock, bored into the Executioner. But he was a tough one. Even while the pain raced through him, Sarai instinctively reached for his enemy, his fingers clawing toward Bolan's eyes like steel talons.

It gave him no choice. The man wouldn't be taken alive. Bolan raised the Beretta and fired at point-blank range. Jacques Sarai dropped like stone to the floor, and Bolan scrambled to his feet.

Stefanie Heidegger stared at him, recognition finally dawning. "What are you doing here?"

"Saving your life," Bolan replied, glancing down at the fallen security man. "From the looks of things."

"I could have handled it myself," she said.

Bolan looked her up and down. The scant robe revealed a soft, lush figure that didn't seem very combat-ready. Her eyes were frightened, flicking from left to right. She looked beautiful, enticing, but she didn't look like a woman who could have handled the situation herself.

Except for the hand that dipped into her robe pocket.

"You carrying a bazooka in there?" he asked.

Her hand came out slowly, holding a cartridge pen.

Bolan smiled. "What were you going to do? Write him a letter?" But he studied the pen carefully. He'd seen dozens of similar items in the past. Take the top off and the nib could be a deadly weapon. A spring-loaded mechanism inside could shoot a chemical-laced dart. Given Stefanie's expertise, it made sense to have such a weapon around. But she hadn't used it on the man when he was obviously forcing himself on her.

"You screamed," Bolan said. "You couldn't use it."

She lowered her head and then looked at the still form of Jacques Sarai. "You're right," she said. "I couldn't use it on him. Not yet."

"What is it? BZ? CS?"

"A bit of both, actually," she admitted. "And something more. It's called Sandman. Two seconds and you're knocked out."

"Sandman," Bolan said. "Acid Bath. Sounds like they had you build up quite an arsenal."

She nodded.

"Potent stuff, if you've got the willpower to use it," Bolan said. "But even if you can't pull the trigger yourself, you can still fight them."

Stefanie was numb, dancing around the edge of shock. A moment ago she'd almost been a victim. Now she had to confront the man who'd come to her aid. But what did he want in return? In her world everybody wanted something.

"You came back. Why?"

"We made a deal," Bolan replied. "I came back to see if you're ready to keep it."

She nodded. Then her eyes looked at a faraway landscape, the road she'd traveled that had ended here in Tongasa, Bolan thought. If anyone knew of how vulnerable her position was, it was Stefanie Heidegger. At last.

Bolan walked over to the door, closed it, then led her to a table by the front window of the flat where he could see down into the street below. It was deserted.

"Cards on the table," he said, sitting across from her.

"What do you mean?"

He put the Beretta on the tabletop and slid it to the right. "If we're going to talk freely, it'll help if we don't have weapons trained on each other."

She nodded and slid the cartridge pen onto the table.

"There's not much time," he said. "I've got to get some answers from you. But first, I've got some for you."

He told her about Kyle Vincent and the information that Hal Brognola had dug up from Justice Department files. The CIA rogue had first recruited Wolf Heidegger for the Agency for a drug and behavior modification program that had trained agents to live and work behind enemy lines. Then the CIA supershrink had turned him into a double agent working for the KGB. When suspicion had fallen on Kyle Vincent as the possible leader of the spy ring, he'd diverted attention to Wolf Heidegger, manipulating events so that a kill team could take out both Heidegger and his KGB handlers.

With Heidegger and the ring silenced, Kyle Vincent was able to masquerade as a patriot a while longer... and go to work on Wolf's daughter.

"He was my friend," she said. "Vincent did so much for me in the beginning."

"He was your father's friend, too," Bolan replied. "Until it became more convenient to kill him."

Bolan gave her the information straight, painting a true portrait of Kyle Vincent, Graham Montgomery and Wadante. He pulled no punches in reciting the litany of the triad's atrocities before and after they'd taken Leon Drew.

"I was starting to know these things myself," she told him, "but I didn't want to admit that... that—"

"That you've been living a lie all this time," Bolan concluded. "Admit it now, and do something about it. You can help undo some of the things you've started."

"Can I get asylum if I cooperate?" she said.

Bolan shook his head. "The U.S. embassy's closed. The French embassy's a dangerous place to be at the moment. There's really nowhere to turn to..."

"Except to you," she said.

"Right," Bolan said. "All you've got on your side is me. But at least I won't plan on killing you at the end of the operation like the rest of your pals will. Help me and I'll get you out of this alive. Along with a lot of innocent people."

"And without my help?" Stefanie leaned forward on the table, cradling her chin in her hands and looking more like a coed in a dormitory than a chemist in a war-torn country.

"Without it you've got no one looking out for you." The warrior gestured toward Jacques Sarai. "Except for his kind."

"What do you want me to give you?"

"The antidote to Acid Bath for a start," Bolan said. "The sample I took with me last time is being examined by the government. But I imagine there might be other variations of the drug that require different antidotes."

"There are," she admitted.

"I'll want all the antidotes, then," Bolan said. "And I want to know any other chemical weapons you've developed, whether you can get some of them out, and if not, when I can send some people in to take them."

"Loot the laboratory and they'll know pretty damn fast."

"By then there won't be much they can do about it." Bolan continued with his checklist. "We'll also want protective devices for our people. And we'll want to spike the remaining munitions—"

"So if Wadante's men use the weapons—"

"They'll be using them on themselves," Bolan said.

"You don't ask for much."

"I take what I need, and give what I can. When it's life or death, there's damn little to negotiate about."

"I'll take life." Stefanie began to tell him about the chemical weaponry she'd been working on in addition to the Acid Bath drugs.

It matched with the limited intel that Montrose had been able to feed Bolan about the CW capacity Wadante was trying to build. If the Acid Bath program failed, the Tongasan strongman planned on having the great equalizer in his hand. He might not be able to buy, steal or build nukes, but chemical weapons always posed a significant threat.

A threat Bolan had to meet.

According to Stefanie, a witch's brew of chemical agents was stockpiled inside the labs at the Ministry of Culture—bombs, canisters, mortars, aerosol sprays, grenades and gas guns, vials. The payloads could be delivered on the battlefield or in the backyard.

Stefanie proved to be an eager conspirator. Death was always a great convincer. When they were finished talking, Bolan had a good handle on Wadante's operation.

Then he turned to the heavy Tongasan security man and slung one arm over his shoulder.

"What are you going to do with him?" she asked. "What if they come looking for him?"

"I'm going to take him for a swim in the river," Bolan said. "It'll be some time before they find his body. Don't worry about people looking for him. With what he had in mind for you, I doubt he told anyone where he was going tonight." He dragged the man to the door and said, "Besides, there will be some people watching you from here on in. Friends. If anyone starts something with you, they'll finish it."

The Executioner carried the deadweight down to the street and spirited the carcass through the deserted shadows. Upon reaching the river that ran by the edge of the city, Bolan removed the man's security uniform, weighted down the body and sent him on his last patrol.

15

The man in the Tongasan Security Squad uniform marched into the Ministry of Culture as if he owned the building. He ignored the sleepy-eyed soldier manning the night desk by the front door, moving past him as if he had no time to waste on minor officials.

Ico's natural air of command, along with the Tongasan SS uniform he wore, put the deskman on the defensive. But just the same, he trailed after Ico, who was jangling a heavy brass ring of keys in his hand.

"You must sign in—"

Ico snapped his head around and glared at the man. "I *must not* sign in," he snapped. "What I must do is equip my men for a secret operation that is being launched even as we speak." He turned right and headed for the staircase farthest from the guardroom, which was occupied by the usual contingent of elite card players.

"No one told me!" the man protested, catching up to Ico's long strides.

"It's classified," Ico replied. "Only those with a need to know are told about such things and only at the right time. And that time is now." He gripped the man's shoulder and said, "I need your help. Follow me."

The lateness of the hour had dulled the clerk's sensibilities. And Ico's no-nonsense approach left him no time to think. He found himself tagging along behind the tall Tongasan up the staircase, then down the hall to the lab. Ico swiftly unlocked the door to the lab with the keys Stefanie Heidegger had passed to them. He stepped inside, then glanced toward the back of the room where a number of crates were positioned off to the side.

"Good," Ico said. "It's ready just as they said it would be. Help me carry some of this outside."

"I should be at my desk—"

"You *should* be shot for not following my orders!"

"But it's not in my authority to even leave my post—"

"It is now," Ico said. "The Security Squad always had top priority." When the man still seemed hesitant, Ico patted his holstered side arm. "This is your authority. Now come on."

The man nodded, realizing that any further orders would come at gunpoint.

Ico headed toward the nearest wooden crate and carefully raised one end, waiting for the dragooned soldier to carry his share. Together they brought the crate down the stairs and out to a jeep that had been "liberated" for the evening from a bar full of FTL soldiers. In the cab sat two men in FTL regular uniforms.

"All right you two," Ico said, "don't make this man do all the work. Lend a hand."

Together the quartet moved back inside the Ministry of Culture. They carefully removed the stock of chemical ordnance and protective suits that Stefanie Heidegger had put aside for them, piling them into the back of the truck.

The truck was parked in the glare of lights from the ministry's entrance. The brightness made the best possible camouflage. If anyone bothered to watch them, it would look very much like an official operation.

At the moment the midnight requisition team was being watched closely by Mack Bolan and a handful of Kesho Dawa guerrillas who had infiltrated the area. Bolan sat behind the wheel of a jeep that had also been stolen for the night. It hadn't been hard. These days the most common troop movements of the FTL took place from bar to bar.

The Executioner breathed out the tension as he watched Ico's men finish loading the truck. The operation appeared to be proceeding smoothly. But just in case, Bolan's hand rested on the 9 mm Sola submachine gun sitting on the seat beside him.

One way or the other they were going to leave the ministry with the goods.

The final battle was approaching. While the FTL troops were preparing to take the war to the guerrillas, the Kesho Dawas were getting ready to take to the streets once again. One of the key elements in the battle would be Montgomery's newly formed hunter battalion. It was gearing up for an all-out assault on the Kesho Dawas, a major punitive expedition. All they had to do was find the guerrillas.

And Bolan was going to give them a road map. To the wrong place.

Even now the disinformation campaign he and André Montrose had formed was in the works. If Montgomery followed that map, the odds for the Kesho Dawas taking the capital would increase.

If not, all hell would break loose. And a large part of that hell was contained in the crates loaded on Ico's truck.

Bolan breathed easy when he saw the tall guerrilla salute the FTL soldier he'd recruited for his "classified" mission to remove the chemical munitions.

It was over.

The Executioner started the engine, then followed Ico's vehicle through the back streets toward the river where a Kesho Dawa crew waited to unload the cargo.

THE FRENCH EMBASSY was a lime-colored mansion that sat like a ripe fruit in the sun, surrounded by gardens and pools and spired fencing. Iron balconies ran along the front of the mansion, then traced a zigzag path along several connecting wings with brightly painted shuttered windows.

From the outside it was picture perfect, looking as peaceful as it did in the colonial days.

Inside, however, all was not well. The acting ambassador had closeted himself in his office, avoiding contact with his own subordinates as well as official

Tongasans. His whole purpose in life was to come down on the right side when the smoke cleared.

Pierre Foucault, on the other hand, had descended upon the embassy like de Gaulle himself, intent on shaping the fate of France and Tongasa alike. He'd made a fortune in the bargain. The tusks harvested by Montgomery's Kenyan expedition were even now on their way to being processed overseas through the smuggling network coordinated by Foucault and some low-ranking staff members of the embassy.

But more than ivory had brought Foucault to Tongasa. He'd come to deal in lives. At the moment André Montrose's was at stake. Foucault's solid relationship with Wadante gave him considerable clout in the embassy. That clout gave him the virtual run of the place, making it easy for him to have Montrose's office bugged.

He smiled as he sat in his luxuriously appointed salon, listening to André's conversation, which was being recorded for posterity on a small deck. The tape would eventually go to the Tongasans and seal his doom. For now, however, Foucault was content to eavesdrop for more information to turn over to Montgomery and his FTL henchmen.

"It won't be long now," Montrose said. "Soon this madness will end."

"You place a lot of faith in an army that's probably not even coming," a second man observed.

Foucault identified the second voice as Robert Valois, Montrose's cultural affairs assistant. Machine gun culture, Foucault thought.

"Oh, but the mercenaries will arrive," Montrose argued. "I'm convinced. So are the Kesho Dawas. People who should know—these people know the mercs are coming. I've heard it from too many reliable sources to think otherwise."

"I still say Baptiste isn't the kind of man to employ mercenaries," Valois replied. "Not after all the things he's said. It's not what he stands for."

"Yes, well, if he's more interested in standing than falling, he'll need such men. No, I believe what I heard. The mercs will arrive. Tonight."

"Where?"

"The highlands."

"Even if they come," Valois said, "what can they do?"

"My friend, they can link up with the Kesho Dawas and launch a joint attack against Monty's strike force, getting rid of him once and for all."

"Who are the mercenaries?"

"Americans, I believe," Montrose said. "And South Africans. Tried men. They'll offer Wadante some real competition for a change."

"If they come, what shall we do when they arrive?"

"Why, my good man, like all good diplomats, we'll close our eyes and duck."

ONE FLOOR BELOW, André Montrose shook his head from left to right as he spoke. His conspiratorial look matched that of his assistant Valois, who had little patience for spook-speak but knew he had to play out the game.

Montrose continued the charade for Foucault's benefit. For days now he and Valois had been subtly making sure the FTL allies in the embassy were able to eavesdrop on conversations about the mercenaries that Baptiste was supposedly bringing in.

Kesho Dawa guerrillas had also let it slip to known FTL infiltrators in the movement that help was coming from a large group of mercenaries flying into Tongasa. Soon the FTL grapevine was abuzz with news that a foreign airdrop was in the works. Special forces mercenaries were coming into the highlands to link up with the Kesho Dawas.

Word also spread through the Tongasan villages until it was practically taken for granted that someone was coming to free them. Like the second coming of Arthur, a king would come to save them just because they needed a king. A great warrior.

The warrior was indeed in Tongasa. But, in large part, his invading army was made up of ghosts.

Even so, Montgomery had prepared to meet them, posting recon teams in the highlands, ''guerrilla'' recruits in the villages and men like Pierre Foucault in the embassy. He would be ready if they came.

JEAN-CLAUDE BAPTISTE peered through the bush at the dark, shuttered streets of Tongasa. Even through the darkness, through the vision of his memory, the leader of the guerrillas saw a different city entirely.

It was a city with an industrious population, with contacts in Europe and throughout East Africa, a city where the citizens could walk unafraid of their own government.

It hadn't been so long ago that Baptiste had walked the streets of Tongasa as a free man, and soon he'd walk those streets again or die trying. One way or the other he'd be free again.

So would the guerrillas gathered around him.

The guerrillas were in a strong position. If any FTL troops came after them, they would find themselves walking through a guerrilla minefield. But hopefully it wouldn't come to that. Hopefully they could attack at the FTL's most vulnerable moment—when Montgomery's hunter battalion was lured out of the city.

Soon they would move, Baptiste thought. Soon they would be up to full strength.

The guerrillas had been making for the capital for days now, moving in small bands. Each group sent out a small recon team toward the edge of the jungle and linked up with the Kesho Dawa runners who moved from base to base. Then, like creatures of the night, they waited for the chance to move against their prey.

They waited for the time when their leader could show his claws.

INSECTS WHIRRED around the Executioner as he sat on the moonlit hilltop looking down into the city. Something scurried through the woods to his left. Probably one of the ring-tailed genets that populated the area, Bolan thought. A good number of the nocturnal catlike carnivores had wound up on many a Kesho Dawa cookfire during the early days.

The warrior waited until the sounds diminished, then reached out for the suitcase-sized satcom gear that had come in on the airdrop with him when he'd returned to Tongasa.

In the distance the capital looked almost serene, the scattered lights from the government buildings casting a halo upon Tongasa. But halos were in short supply among the FTL leadership.

He raised the suitcase lid of the parabolic satellite transceiver, unfolded the antenna and aimed it toward the military satellite in geosynchronous orbit above the Indian Ocean.

The phone unit had normal voice, scrambler or encrypted keyboard communications that would bounce off the satellite and connect him to Hal Brognola in real time.

But tonight Bolan used normal voice mode. The chance that anyone in the FTL would pick up the signal was small, but even if they did, it would prop up the disinformation campaign in the works.

Bolan keyed the proper code numbers and raised Brognola, who was coordinating outside support aboard the customized Justice Department jet flying over Kenyan airspace.

"HF-1, this is Executive. HF-1, this is Executive," Bolan said.

The head Fed acknowledged the transmission, then said, "We're waiting for the business plan, Executive. It's your call, over."

"Commence MAN-K," Bolan announced. "I repeat, commence MAN-K."

"MAN-K is in the air," Brognola replied. "MAN-K is in the air."

Bolan signed off. Operation Mannequin had begun. Their part was done. It was up to the toy soldiers from here on in.

ONE HOUR LATER and two hundred miles to the west, two unmarked C-130s flew north to south across the highlands of Tongasa. They flew low and slow, easily spotted by any FTL observers posted in the area. And there definitely were some FTL teams nosing around in the past few days. A group of Kesho Dawa rangers had seen the FTL recon teams slicing through the wilderness toward the highlands. They'd let them pass so that the FTL spotters could radio back to the capital when the airborne mercenaries arrived.

The aircraft made their drop shortly before midnight. The jumpmasters pushed first one soldier, then another out the jump doors.

Stone-faced and silent paratroopers rained soundlessly from the planes, their rigid figures plummeting swiftly until the static lines tripped their chutes. The chutes flared, their silhouettes marked easily against the night as they dropped toward the dark wilderness below.

Minutes later, in the presidential palace, Graham Montgomery received the radio reports from his recon teams with divine fire in his eyes, like a hermit who'd finally heard the word from on high. The airborne force had just arrived. FTL recon teams had been able to watch them from the distance and even now were moving toward the LZ in order to radio further reports and pinpoint the area.

It was time for him to take the stage, time to end Wadante's endless carping about the debacle Montgomery had caused.

Time to end the life of the man who'd almost single-handedly derailed the Acid Bath program.

But now it could be saved. Now the hunter battalion could do its work.

The mercs had arrived after all, landing in the highlands just as the rumors had proclaimed. They'd link up with forces all right—but not just the Kesho Dawas.

Montgomery had been waiting. His men were on standby. So were the Puma and Alouette crews.

He gave the word for the battalion to move out. There would be two salients. One was a land-based phalanx of armored vehicles and jeeps to meet the mercs as they headed south. The other was airborne, and Montgomery would be with them.

AS THE ARMORED COLUMN wound out of the city and the Pumas flew overhead, their rotors drumming against the treetops, Mack Bolan followed their progress. He wasn't alone. Hundreds of pairs of eyes looked up from their hiding spots in the woods.

Montgomery had taken the bait.

He would find that the mercenary paratroopers really had dropped into the highlands. The black flight operation brought in untraceable, nameless mercs, who wouldn't run no matter what happened.

The airborne "mercs" were mannequins, camouflage-painted dummies who'd naturally made the night jump without protest. It was a page taken from the Spetznas' handbook. The Soviet special forces routinely dropped fake paratroopers deep behind enemy lines—causing confusion, chaos and panic. A few teams of real troops on the ground would lend credence to the paratroopers, raising enough hell for a division of dummies.

The tactic might not work against a sophisticated country with troops and early-warning systems on their borders, but against a backwater battalion it would do just fine. Seeing was believing, and until Montgomery's men reached the drop zone, they'd believe they had the mercs and the Kesho Dawas cornered.

By then it would be all over.

Bolan glanced over at Ico and Baptiste and nodded. The three men stood soundlessly and moved through the jungle to join the other Kesho Dawa guerrillas.

"Let's move," Bolan said.

16

The truck depot was manned by a small force of FTL soldiers who considered night duty a reward. Especially tonight. With Montgomery out of town hunting down the rebels, there seemed little for them to do but kill time or sleep.

The only one who really had to stay awake was the gate house guard, who sat inside a small white building positioned between the exit and entrance gates, logging in all movements of FTL trucks.

The vehicles came and went at all hours, ferrying stolen relief supplies, furniture and gadgetry confiscated from the wealthier mansions, and troops coming back from the field.

A square splash of light escaped from the gate house window, joined by floodlights from under the eaves, making the steepled building an oasis among the darkness. Inside, an FTL guard sat hypnotized by a *Playboy* centerfold, just one of many Western products confiscated by the FTL.

He looked annoyed as a pair of headlights spiked the darkness. Engine groaning, a canvas-covered truck pulled up alongside the gate house.

The guard grabbed his clipboard, opened the sliding doors of the gate house and stepped out onto the concrete platform, ready to check out the driver as the truck rolled forward and stopped in front of the wooden barricade.

It was routine.

So routine that the sight of the white face didn't trouble him at first. Les Affreux came and went almost at will, never signing out the trucks, often bringing them back in beyond repair. But the guard suddenly realized that most of the mercenaries would be out on the hunt tonight.

He reached for his side arm, but a round from Mack Bolan's silenced Beretta reached him first. The man's legs crumpled beneath him. His falling body was caught by one of the Kesho Dawa guerrillas who'd climbed off the back of the truck.

The body was hauled inside the vehicle and replaced by a guerrilla wearing an FTL uniform, who stepped into the gate house and pressed the button that raised the wooden barricade.

Bolan drove the truck forward into the garage and rolled to a stop in the center of the cavernous truck bay. A half-dozen guerrillas slipped out of the back and headed for the vehicles parked nearby. They climbed onto the running boards, slipped in behind the seats and switched on the ignitions. Another guerrilla headed straight for the Berliet VXB armored vehicle, which looked like a metal cigar box fitted with a bulletproof windshield and a bulldozer blade.

The movement of the guerrillas attracted the notice of the handful of FTL soldiers who were milling around a long table against the wall that was littered with coffee cups and flasks. The soldiers glared at the newcomers with practiced resentment, wondering if their presence meant more work for them. But then, as more guerrillas spilled from the back of Bolan's truck, they caught on.

"Kesho Dawas!" one of the FTL soldiers shouted, unslinging his submachine gun.

Bolan kicked open his door and hosed the soldiers with a burst from his submachine gun. The 9 mm barrage kicked the soldiers back toward the wall where they landed in a crumpled heap.

The rest of the Kesho Dawas moved back and forth from Bolan's truck, distributing the cargo of machine guns, rocket launchers and explosives to the other vehicles. Within minutes the convoy was ready.

The vehicles rolled through the gates and spread out into the streets. At various points the trucks slowed to a crawl, waiting for groups of guerrillas to emerge from the shadows.

The Kesho Dawas poured out of safehouses they'd infiltrated during the past few days, some of them climbing aboard the truck while others removed some of the weapons and carried them back into the shadows where they'd prepared for the upcoming battle. Machine gun emplacements were set up beneath buildings and on rooftops to control the streets during the fighting.

With Bolan at the wheel of the lead truck, the convoy carried its deadly cargo toward its ultimate destination—the presidential palace. There a large concentration of FTL soldiers manned trenches that were dug just outside the palace, following the contours like a sandbagged moat.

Surrounded by the high iron fences, the palace was a deadly zoo where the worst beasts of the FTL prowled behind the gates.

TWO HUNDRED MILES away Graham Montgomery moved in the darkness through the Tongasan wilderness. Moonlight speared through the forest clearings from time to time and cast brambled shadows on the ground. But most of the going was through heavily wooded areas with little moonlight spilling through the treetop canopy.

The Briton was following one of the FTL recon teams that had popped flares for the landing zone and now led them toward the mercenary paratroopers.

The entire hunter battalion had disembarked from the Pumas and was now spread out behind him. There would be no escape for the foreign mercs.

This was Montgomery's kind of war. Head-on and to the end. The battalion would make contact and exterminate both the mercs and the Kesho Dawa units. Then, with Tongasa looking more stable in the eyes of the world, the Acid Bath program could begin again.

The brush grabbed at Montgomery's night-black garb as he closed in on the area the recon teams had pinpointed as the paratroopers' drop zone. When they came to the edge of a clearing, one of the guides tapped him on the shoulder and pointed skyward.

Montgomery saw the shadowy form of a paratrooper hanging from the upper branches, his chute hopelessly snarled. His legs hung down perfectly still. Playing possum, he thought. Other paratroopers were also caught in some of the trees. They, too, were still.

Montgomery smiled. He raised his 7.62 mm FAL rifle and trained it on the nearest paratrooper. He looked around to see that his men were in position, then triggered a burst. The slugs smashed into the paratrooper, making a chipping sound as the man danced and spun in the trees.

The Briton's burst ignited a barrage of autofire as all around him the FTL hunters opened up, peppering the trees and the underbrush ahead of them. Severed arms and legs dropped from the trees in incredible numbers.

And then the strangeness of it all finally registered on Montgomery. There had been no return fire, and there had been that strange chipping sound when the bullets had struck the paratroopers.

It was the sound of wood. Splintering wood.

"Hold your fire!" Montgomery shouted.

He thrashed through the bush, ran toward the closest tree and looked up at the first trooper he'd opened up on. The man's right leg was sawed off, half of his torso was missing and his wooden, camouflaged face gazed down at him, a grim smile painted on it.

Montgomery looked all around him at the bizarre masquerade of carnage. Several paratroopers had fallen to the ground, perfectly bloodless and stock still. Their grotesquely positioned bodies looked like a harvest of phantoms in the beam of his flashlight.

The light splayed across a gallery of hideously painted faces—totally undisturbed by the fact that most of their bodies were missing.

"Bloody fucking dummies!" he roared.

"What do you mean?" the guide asked, catching up to the Briton and following the beam of light as it illuminated the wooden faces.

"I mean us and them," Montgomery said. "Fucking dummies. The mercenaries are mannequins. Nothing but mannequins. It was a fake airdrop."

"But we saw some of them moving," the man protested.

"Just enough to make it look good," Montgomery said. "They plant a few Kesho Dawa teams in the area to make a bit of noise and run. They're probably out of here by now—"

Several horrendous explosions from the landing zone proved him wrong.

"The choppers!" he shouted. "They're after the choppers..."

Montgomery heard four more blasts in succession and then saw a fireball rising skyward as the gasoline tanks erupted. One after the other the bright tongues of flame lapped up at the darkness.

And suddenly his perfect war was coming apart all around him. He ran back through the forest with his men to see how many helicopters they could salvage.

BOLAN WHEELED the lead truck down the Boulevard des Martyrs, temporarily separating himself from the rest of the convoy. Then he turned down the side street where the French embassy was located and slowly drove past the long iron fence. He searched for the uppermost windows on the left side of the mansion. An unused storeroom, Montrose had said.

Both windows of the usually darkened storeroom were unshuttered and lighted. That was their agreed-upon signal that Montrose had successfully smuggled Stefanie Heidegger into the embassy and that Montrose's GIGN operatives were in position on the roof-tops closest to the presidential palace.

It was a go.

Though Bolan had faith in the Kesho Dawas as fighters, he knew a few well-placed *gigenes* could make all the difference in the early stages of the battle. They were past masters of the weaponry the guerrillas had secreted on the rooftop bunkers closest to the palace.

Bolan continued down the side street, turned right at the corner, then joined up with the remaining trucks that were cruising slowly toward the presidential palace.

The VXB and two other vehicles had veered off toward the Ministry of Culture building a half mile away.

The Executioner moved his truck to the front of the convoy and proceeded to the front gate. As he neared the gate, he wheeled to the left and drove parallel to the fencing. Coming almost to a stop, he spun the wheel hard away from the fence, shifted into reverse and eased the back of the truck toward the iron fence.

A half-dozen other trucks split up on both sides of the gate and performed similar maneuvers. Inside the truck beds, the waiting guerrillas manned an assortment of machine guns, shotguns and grenade launchers.

Bolan slung his Sola submachine gun over his shoulder, grabbed the Hilton MPRG shotgun from the passenger seat and climbed down from the truck cab. He rapped the side of the truck as he moved to the back. Other drivers followed suit. A handful of guerrillas jumped down from the back of each vehicle, wearing a mixture of khaki and black fatigues.

"Look smart," Bolan directed. "You're in the FTL now."

Ico moved up beside him. "For how long?" he asked, a grim smile on his lips.

"As long as we can stand it," Bolan replied. "We'll have about a minute before they know who we really are."

Ico nodded and moved down the line, speaking to some of the Kesho Dawa soldiers as he headed toward the gate.

Jean-Claude Baptiste appeared on the opposite side of the gate, commanding the Kesho Dawas on the right side. He walked with the crisp stride of a military professional, and with the burning eyes of a man who saw the end of the battle in sight. And victory.

It was the only way to go, Bolan thought, whether that vision was misplaced or not. The fiery look was contagious, spreading from face to face of the men who followed Baptiste.

The guerrillas marched in formation like FTL troops and lined up just outside the front gate. While waiting for the other guerrillas to reach them, they faced away from the palace as if they were preparing to repel any invaders.

To the men stirring in the trenches, it looked as if a group of troopers had been summoned to the palace to reinforce them. In that critical moment when the blue-uniformed presidential guard was off balance—and a bit thankful for the new arrivals—the Kesho Dawas spun around, crouched and speared their weapons through the iron fencing.

Bolan rested the MPRG stock on his shoulder, aimed at the wall above the trench full of FTL troops and shouted, "Fire!" He triggered a 12-gauge special purpose shotgun load, thumping a CS cartridge into the wall just above the trench. The cartridge burst and sent the first of many chemical clouds down upon the FTL.

To his left and right automatic weapons opened up, pouring a barrage of lead toward the trenches. The machine guns mounted on the tailgates of the trucks blasted heavy-metal volleys into the walls.

The fusillade kept the FTL soldiers pinned while Bolan and a number of guerrillas fired off grenades and rocket launchers, sending smoke, gas and high-explosive rounds crashing against the palace facade.

As the gas and smoke choked them, the soldiers stood and made a run for it—right into the scything blades of autofire. Half of them dropped back into the trenches, leaking blood. The others scrambled madly from the trenches and clawed their way onto the grass, heading for the guerrillas, or the imagined safety of the guardhouse, which had been in flames since the beginning of the attack. Regardless of their destination, few of the FTL soldiers made it very far.

Bolan moved up and down the line, firing his submachine gun through the fence posts, now and then aiming another CS cartridge at the trenches.

During a brief lull in the battle, the Executioner glanced back at the houses in the distance. When Wadante had cleared away the block closest to the palace, many of the remaining houses were abandoned or taken over by squatters. The collection of colonial-style buildings were ripe for occupation by the GIGN operatives.

The next stage of the attack depended on them.

Bolan and the Kesho Dawas could sustain the assault on the FTL ground troops, but right now they needed longer arms to reach the rooftop helipad.

"Where the hell are they?" Bolan said aloud.

His answer came a moment later when a trio of warheads streaked across the sky, converging on the fortified rooftop.

Montrose's GIGN operatives had carefully staked out their positions on the upper floors, knocking holes in the rear walls for the backblasts from the LAW 80 and Dragon launchers they'd fired at the top of the palace. HEAT rounds sledgehammered the concrete bastions, sending stone and bone flying into the air. A

HESH round came screaming in for the helipad, the squash-head missile sending shock waves through the platform and making a huge crater.

The Fourth of July had come to Tongasa. Plumes of smoke trailed over the palace grounds, ending in brilliant flashes. Concrete danced into the air as murky war clouds billowed over the capital.

While the GIGN team went to work, Bolan broke out the S6 antiriot respirators from the back of his truck and passed them out to the guerrillas. The air cushions of the masks molded to their faces, giving them protection from the smoke and gas swirling around the trenches.

Now that they had softened up the opposition, they had to wade into the smoky hell they'd created.

THE VXB GENDARMERIE armored vehicle stormed past the front of the Ministry of Culture, the machine gunner blasting away at the row of jeeps and trucks parked at the curb. The side door of the armored tin can kicked open and a guerrilla with an Armsel Striker semiautomatic shotgun blasted away at the vehicles. Seconds later the VXB stormed around the corner, leaving behind a row of battered and broken vehicles.

A truckload of SMG-wielding Kesho Dawa guerrillas waited until the VXB rounded the corner before making their mop-up run, opening up on the vehicles that had somehow survived the initial barrage intact. They triggered full-auto blasts at the scattered units of FTL soldiers who came running from the ministry building.

Now that they'd destroyed the vehicles that could have transported reinforcements to the palace, the truck driver stomped on the accelerator and rocketed out of there.

The truck headlights soon flashed across the dull-metal tail end of the VXB, catching up with the vehicle just as it was about to crash through the gates of the presidential palace.

The huge dozer blade smashed into the concrete column that anchored the gate. The column cracked and shuddered, then tilted back, supported by the iron fencing. The VXB backed up, then roared forward once again, toppling the gates.

The guerrillas surged forward, leaving a small rear guard to block the gates with trucks and hold off an FTL counterattack. They followed the VXB, which trampled any FTL soldiers who offered resistance.

Bolan and Jean-Claude Baptiste were the first to leap across the trenches, then storm through the shattered entrance into the palace.

17

André Montrose watched as a dark figure stepped into his office at the embassy, gun in hand. The intruder raised the weapon and aimed at the back of the black leather desk chair by the window where Montrose usually sat. A dim yellow circle of lamplight spilled onto the desk. The rest of the room was dark.

Streaks of flame shot toward the chair as the assassin fired two rounds, which ripped apart the back of the chair and hurled Montrose's linen-stuffed uniform and cap onto the desktop.

Montrose pushed away from the wall and snapped his left foot straight up. His instep caught the intruder under the chin and clacked his teeth together. But the gunman still held on to his weapon.

Hearing more footsteps outside the hallway, Montrose acted by reflex. Rather than try to take the man alive for questioning, he leveled his Manurhin .357 Magnum and squeezed the trigger. The blast from the standard-issue GIGN weapon knocked the assassin off his feet and blew a part of his chest against the wall. He crashed to the floor, a lifeless heap.

One glance told Montrose all he needed to know—the assassin was an FTL trooper who had somehow infiltrated the embassy. He took a step toward the door, the Manurhin stabbing the air in front of him.

"André!" a voice whispered. "It's me. Valois!"

Montrose relaxed and stepped out into the hallway. Valois stood there with a MAT 49 9 mm submachine gun cradled in his arms.

Sounds of battle wafted up from the floors below.

"The guard at the gate has been killed," Valois told him. "The embassy's been penetrated—"

"Foucault's behind this."

"The bastard baron finally shows his fangs," Valois agreed.

Montrose glanced toward the ceiling. Stefanie Heidegger was waiting upstairs, firmly convinced that she was safe under his protection. "First us, then the girl," he said. "Very neat. He gets rid of all of his enemies who know what he's been up to. Then he'll blame it on the Tongasan troops."

"And he comes out of it a hero," Valois added. "Unless we stop him."

Montrose nodded. "Let's check on the girl. I gave my word she'd be safe with us."

Valois turned around, jogged to the end of the corridor and turned the corner that led to the stairwell.

Montrose was several steps behind when a blast of lead punched a hole in the wall at the end of the corridor. "Foucault!" he shouted, spinning and triggering several rounds.

The shots kept Foucault off balance for a moment, but he recovered and leveled his own weapon. Montrose dropped flat on his back, startling Foucault for a split second, forcing him to lower his gunhand.

Valois whipped around the corner and triggered a full-auto burst from the MAT 49. The fusillade hammered Pierre Foucault back down the hall and nailed him to the wall.

Valois extended his compatriot a helping hand, and the two of them raced upstairs to see if the redhaired chemist had escaped Foucault's purge.

"What the hell's going on?" she shouted when they burst into the room. "Who's attacking us?"

"Your friends," Montrose said. Although he was relieved that she was alive, he was still bitter. He'd agreed with Bolan to keep her alive for the part she'd played in helping plan the assault on the palace, but he considered her to be the same stripe as Foucault. "Relax," he soothed. "You're safe as long as I keep my eye on you—and rest assured that will be until the shooting stops."

He peered outside the now-dimmed windows of the storage room and saw a wave of FTL soldiers fleeing the embassy grounds—and mowed down by the GIGN contingent that had returned from the assault on the palace. They had played their part. The rest was up to the American warrior.

"HOLD IT!" Bolan growled, straight-arming Baptiste in the chest, preventing him from bursting into the pitch-black corridor on the top floor.

"Move out of the way," Baptiste commanded. Behind the guerrilla leader stood the Kesho Dawas who'd survived the assault on the trenches and the firefight inside the main entrance. They were spread out on the corridor and down the staircase, eager to follow Baptiste. "We've got them on the run."

"Custer said the same thing just before he led his men to their deaths," Bolan replied. "We've made it this far. Don't throw it away."

The Executioner approached the edge of the corridor. It was long and wide, the main galley that connected the front wing of the palace to the rear and then upstairs to the roof. It was silent. Dead silent.

Baptiste glanced at Ico, who had just pushed through the other guerrillas in time to hear the conversation. He nodded toward Bolan, casting his vote with the Executioner.

"What do you suggest?" Baptiste asked.

"A bit of caution, and a bit of thunder."

Though it looked as if the battle was all but over, the Executioner had survived too many wars to sacrifice himself or the Kesho Dawas. True, many of the FTL soldiers had thrown down their arms and fled as soon as the guerrillas had breached the palace. After mopping up the resistance on the lower floor, the guerrillas had moved to the upper levels, discarding their gas masks on the way. They hadn't encountered any further resistance.

But the dark corridor ahead was a perfect place for an ambush.

Bolan reached into one of the slit pockets in his blacksuit for a 12-gauge StarFlash Muzzle Blast shell and loaded the Hilton MPRG shotgun. "Wait until I fire, then give it everything you got. We'll have about three seconds before they can recover from the flash."

Bolan angled the barrel of the shotgun around the corridor, then pulled the trigger.

The blast rocked the corridor, producing a hellish wall of light that ripped through the darkness. The stun flash leaped from the shotgun barrel like a flamethrower and illuminated the FTL machine gun emplacements that zigzagged halfway down the corridor.

Thunderstruck by the blast, the gunners were poised in suspended motion by the blinding white-hot sparklets. Then they were rocked by a red-hot fusillade of autofire as Ico, Baptiste and the waiting Kesho Dawas unloaded on the troopers. With an ear-shattering war cry that had been building for over a year now, Baptiste led the guerrillas down the hall.

The scattered FTL soldiers who'd recovered quickly enough to return fire took down only three men before they were overrun. The guerrilla fighters passed through the corridor, then streamed toward the rooftop.

CHAOS REIGNED on the palace rooftop as FTL soldiers ran through the ruins in panic. They shot wildly, taking down many of their own comrades before the main body of guerrillas reached them.

President Wadante's huge form thrashed through the darkness, clad in a regal robe. He'd been sleeping when the attack had commenced. Now he looked like an enraged wizard as he swung his walking stick left and right, shouting and cursing his own men as well as the guerrillas who hounded him.

Both he and Kyle Vincent were headed toward the psychologist's Nightfox helicopter. The CIA rogue always kept the chopper at the ready, manned by his own personal pilot. The countercoup taxi service, he called it.

Since the GIGN rocket attack had knocked out the presidential helicopter, the Nightfox was the only way out.

Vincent hurried the Tongasan dictator along, passing through a gauntlet of FTL troopers who were ready to make their last stand. But the heavy-chested tyrant was out of shape; his pleasure-filled reign had taken its toll. Too winded to keep up with Vincent, he fell behind.

The chopper's rotor whirred overhead, kicking up dust and rubble as Vincent climbed into the cabin. Looking back, he saw the throng of guerrillas slicing through the rubble. They were close, too close.

Wadante reached out his hand to the headshrinker, but Vincent pulled it away. "Up," he shouted to the pilot, jerking his thumb into the air. "There's no time. Leave him!"

The pilot nodded. The copter started to rise just as Wadante reached them and jumped for the skids. His heavy weight rocked the Nightfox—until Vincent leaned out the door and pointed his automatic.

"But we're friends," Wadante shouted, "the three of us..."

"To the end," Vincent shouted in agreement. "And this is the end.

Wadante didn't let go.

Vincent pulled the trigger, and a bloody hole appeared in the Tongasan's forehead. He grimaced once, his sharpened teeth cutting through his lips, then dropped away from the aircraft.

BAPTISTE BROKE through the last line of FTL defenders, submachine gun chattering. He ripped a 3-round burst toward Wadante just as the tyrant fell back toward the ground.

The Executioner had been running full speed toward the helicopter when it pushed off from the ground. Now he dived forward and rolled onto his shoulders just as Vincent fired down at him. The slugs chipped into the concrete, tracking him on the ground, but the Executioner kept moving until he was clear of Vincent's line of fire. Then he stood, raised his shotgun and took aim at the pilot. While the guerrillas poured a steady stream of lead at the chopper, Bolan triggered a blast from the shotgun.

The round caught the pilot just under the rim of his helmet, expending all of its energy on impact. The frangible metal-ceramic load exploded the man's braincase.

Suddenly pilotless, the Nightfox swooped crazily and dipped toward the edge of the rooftop. It came down on its nose, crumpling like a tin can against the concrete. The rotors snapped and whirred through the air like free-floating guillotines before the aircraft teetered on the edge, then toppled over the side.

Baptiste's broad-shouldered silhouette moved through the fading dust and smoke. "It's over."

"Not yet," Bolan said. "Not until we get the seal of approval. Until then we're fair game for anyone who can field an army against you."

"The call?" Baptiste asked.

"Yeah, the call. It's time to drop a dime on Uncle Sam."

The two men coordinated the mopping-up action, then dispatched half the guerrilla force to secure the airstrip while the others shored up the defenses of the presidential palace.

Bolan and Ico went to the perimeter gates where a number of Kesho Dawas had fallen in the early stages of battle, downed by the desperate fire of the FTL soldiers in the trenches. Some of them clung awkwardly to the gates, looking inward, as if even in death they were still with the cause.

Bolan retrieved the parabolic transceiver unit from the truck he'd left by the gate, then returned to the front of the palace where Baptiste was helping separate the wounded Kesho Dawas from the dead.

The Executioner set up the satcom unit and linked up with Brognola. "Wadante's out," he told the head Fed. "For good. Baptiste's in control." Then he handed the receiver to the guerrilla leader. "Got a man here who wants to talk to you."

Baptiste spoke for a moment, then signed off and turned to Bolan. "He said the U.S. is prepared to recognize my government and even now is ready to provide any support requested."

"That sounds about right. Just like you and I discussed. So what did you say?"

"I requested assistance—just until we stabilize the government."

Bolan nodded. A joint armada of U.S., British and Kenyan planes had been lined up on the tarmac of a private airstrip in Kenya near Lake Victoria, waiting for the word from Baptiste. Brognola had made sure there were enough supplies, troops and diplomats on hand to bolster Baptiste's government during the first few critical days.

"They'll be here pretty damn soon," Bolan said.

Baptiste looked at the man who had dropped out of the blue just a short time ago and had helped him take the long and bloody steps toward freedom. "It's like a dream. After all this time we're back in Tongasa and the world is ready to recognize my government." He shook his head. "So what now, my friend?"

"So start governing. In the meantime I'll go out and look over the defenses."

THE DAMAGED PUMA flew low over the treetops, smoke billowing out of the tail end.

Graham Montgomery and a dozen troopers had managed to make it back to the capital aboard the battle-shocked aircraft. It shuddered and shook, dropping lower and lower as it neared the palace.

When the pilot saw the ruins on the rooftop—and the reception committee of Kesho Dawa guerrillas—he banked hard to the left, dropping down quickly while machine gun fire riveted into the side of the captain.

He headed for the gate and freedom.

"No," Montgomery said sharply. "Take us down there." He pointed toward a cluster of men on the ground. One man was directing their defenses, positioning trucks near the gate.

"But it's suicide...."

"Take me down," Montgomery ordered, brandishing a 9 mm Browning automatic. "Then you can do what you want." He held the barrel just inches from the pilot's head.

The battle for the palace was over. Wadante had obviously been overrun. But another leader was still alive. The man who had ruined him in England, in Tongasa, in the wilds... The man who had stayed one step ahead of the Briton all along was down there.

Montgomery had one more battle to fight, and for one of them it would be the last.

The pilot swore, but prodded by the gun and by his past experience with Montgomery, he headed toward the center of the palace grounds, away from the fence and the maze of trucks and machine guns.

Montgomery jumped to the ground, followed by two mercs and four troopers who left the aircraft firing.

The Kesho Dawas streamed toward the helicopter. As if by instinct, every man opened up on the intruders, every man charged straight ahead.

Bolan moved with them, diving into the grass as bullets scythed overhead, autofire that was directed at him. He rolled, clutching the shotgun to his chest while the lead carved furrows in the earth.

With the warrior as the main target, the guerrillas were free to pick off the opposition one by one. As his troops were being cut down, Montgomery stood there, shouting like a possessed man, burning through his clips at full-auto.

The helicopter tried to lift off again, but it had nothing left to give. Gasoline was leaking from the tank, and smoke was billowing from the grinding engine. With no hope of escape the rest of the troopers poured out of the aircraft.

Montgomery bellowed at them, directing their attention at Bolan. But there was a heartbeat's delay before they could identify their target. The Executioner stole that sliver of time from them, rolled to his left and came up with the shotgun at his hip.

He fired not at Montgomery, but at the chopper behind him, then dropped to the ground. The shotgun blast ripped into the leaking gas tank, turning the Puma into a metal volcano that consumed the remaining troopers.

The explosion lifted Montgomery off his feet, his arms spreading wide as he sailed through the air. Then what was left of the Englishman and the Acid Bath program tumbled to the ground in flames.

The Executioner got up and walked toward the gate.

GOLD EAGLE

GOLD EAGLE action/adventure books are now available in stores each month at a new time.

Look for The Executioner and GOLD EAGLE's new miniseries: SURVIVAL 2000, SOLDIERS OF WAR, TIME WARRIORS and AGENTS on the 16th of every month in your favorite retail outlet.

We hope that this new schedule is convenient for you. Please note that there may be slight variations in on-sale dates in your area due to differences in shipping and handling.